THREE'S THE CHARM

Maths, Books Three

P.A. Friday

James, Laurie, and Al are settling into a surprisingly easily life as a triad. Finally, things seem to be going well for them. But when an unscrupulous journalist takes advantage of Al's blossoming film career and the men's unusual relationship to write an exposé article, cracks begin to show. Can the three survive with their love, their careers, and even their sanity intact?

A NineStar Press Publication

Published by NineStar Press
P.O. Box 91792,
Albuquerque, New Mexico, 87199 USA.
www.ninestarpress.com

Three's the Charm

Printed in the USA
First Edition
February, 2018

Print ISBN: 978-1-948608-01-5

Also available in eBook, ISBN: 978-1-948608-00-8

Warning: This book contains sexually explicit content, which may only be suitable for mature readers, and references to sexual assault.

For Sam, who is wonderful

Acknowledgements

Many thanks are due to BJ for her (as always) amazing editing support, and Rosemary for betaing this story and reassuring me it was worth offering to the world.

Even more thanks than usual, actually, to BJ and the rest of Nine Star Press for putting up with me during the editing process as my deteriorating health made things awkward.

And last but not least, love to my family, especially Cameron and my James, who make my life worth living. You are amazing, and I adore you.

Chapter One

AL

The text was brief and to the point.

I hope you're behaving yourself. L.

Al glared at his phone, as if it were his boyfriend Laurie himself. Up until that point, he'd been fairly successful at forgetting that he'd been driven to the point of madness the night before by his lovers, who had made him beg and then refused to allow him the satisfaction he was craving. Okay, that 'forgetting' bit wasn't entirely true. He'd managed to *deal* with the fact that he was absolutely fucking desperate for a wank, or to get off in some form or other. And then bloody Laurie sent that, just reminding him. Rubbing it in.

Al wanted to rub one off, not have things rubbed in. But Laurie, who was not 'just' a boyfriend but—when they both chose—his Dominant, had ordered him not to. To wait for this evening. Scowling so hard at his phone that his boss, Fenella, asked him what the matter was ("Nothing"), he sent a one-word reply.

Yes.

There was silence for an hour. Laurie was probably giving a lecture at the university about filmography or something. Probably doing it well, too—Al had been to a couple of Laurie's lectures in the past, and he was a good speaker, and knowledgeable. Al should know, as well: he was a prominent short film-maker on a minor level, though it was not a career which allowed him to devote himself to it full-time. Hence the job in the wine shop. During the text silence from his boyfriend, therefore, Al talked to various people about wine, advising them on which bottle might suit them best, and managed to ignore the worst of his frustration. Then the phone buzzed again.

Are you hard? L.

Al seethed. Well, if he hadn't been before, he was now. He was bloody hard and fucking desperate. Laurie knew it—he knew precisely what he was doing, damn him. Al was tempted not to answer, to just leave Laurie hanging. But on the other hand, Laurie would be in charge once he got home. Provoking him to further teasing was a seriously bad plan. Hating his boyfriend, he sent the same one-word answer.

Yes.

The 'fuck you' wasn't explicitly written afterwards, but Al was pretty sure Laurie would get that too. Ruffled, he texted James. James, his other boyfriend. Laurie's boyfriend, too.

Your boyfriend is a fucking sadist.

Al smiled apologetically at Fen, who was looking unimpressed by the amount of texting going on in work time.

"There's no one needing serving at the moment," he offered.

She snorted and shook her head. "I suppose you're texting your many partners," she said, trying to sound grumpy but not quite managing it.

As far as Fen was concerned—and it was fairly close to the truth—Al slept with pretty much anyone who offered. He certainly had sex with a lot of people, but not only did he live with James and Laurie, he was also in love with them, which made rather a lot of difference. And, he admitted grumpily, the sex was best with them. Partly because Laurie was the best Dom Al had ever come across, and the only one he'd thoroughly trust with the submissive part of himself; and partly because...well, (a) they were both bloody marvellous in bed, and (b) all right, yes, because he was in love with them and it turned out that that did make a difference, just as everyone claimed. Damn them all.

His phone buzzed again.

Needing a wank? J.

Al had the distinct temptation to smash his phone hard against the counter. James was supposed to be showing a bit of sympathy. Which that was not.

Fuck off.

He got another hour, that time. An hour in which to calm down and to think about wine, and talk sensibly to a customer about which white wine might be the optimal choice to go with a nice fish dinner ("What sort of fish?" "Dead," said the customer, helpfully.)

It was Laurie, again, when the text came.

You're going to have to beg. L.

Al hated how much that turned him on. How much he wanted to be on his knees to Laurie, pleading to be allowed to come. Hated the visions which were flooding his brain after reading it. Fen was giving him a peculiar look, and he excused himself to the toilet. Not to touch—he knew better than that—but to try to compose himself a bit. He could hardly serve customers with a raging hard-on, and at the moment all he could think about was sex. Fuck. Bloody, fucking Laurie. Fuck. Al pushed a hand firmly (painfully firmly) between his black jeans-clad legs, squeezed his eyes shut, and tried to think about other things. Awful things. Running out of money at the end of the month. Stepping in a deep puddle and getting a trainerful of water. Anything. Anything but the thought of Laurie making him beg. Jesus. Eventually, he knew he'd have to come out or face Fen's wrath.

"Sorry," he said apologetically. "Not feeling my best."

"Hmm." Fen's lack of belief would have been mortifying at any other time, but at the moment, Al was too busy trying to deal with his rebellious cock.

You're hot on your knees. J.

Al hadn't even heard that text come in. He'd picked up the phone to check the time—to see how long it was before he could go home and persuade his boyfriends (his absolute bastard boyfriends) to allow him to get off. He'd not replied to Laurie's last text—potentially dangerous in itself, but he was damned if he was going to plead over his phone. Bad enough that he knew bloody well he'd break down and do it in person the first second he saw Laurie; he was not going to humiliate himself in writing as well. And now James, too. James, who knew him too damn well, and knew what a text like that would do.

Thought I told you to fuck off, he wrote.

The response was quick; presumably James was home from work.

Sorry. Thought you asked me to fuck you. *Or was that last night? J.*

It wasn't murder if your boyfriends had asked for it, was it? Al had a sudden memory of the previous evening, where he had indeed done as James had suggested. And James had acted like he was going to give in, and then not done so. Fucking tease.

Al gave an involuntary moan, and Fen looked at him, eyebrows raised. "Anything wrong?"

"Told you," Al said, hoping he wasn't blushing. "Not feeling great."

Unexpectedly, she looked sympathetic. "You can head home early if you like?"

Oh, bloody hell, that was worst of all. Laurie and James would rip the piss out of him something chronic if they knew about this. Fen offering to send him home early because he was so 'unwell'. He'd never live down the fact that he'd been so desperate for them that he hadn't been able to finish a day's work.

"No," he said, knowing his face was definitely red, and quite probably radish-coloured. "I'm fine. Honestly."

"Okay. Let me know if you need to leave, though, Al. Honestly, you don't have to suffer."

Tell that to my boyfriends, Al thought bitterly. Apparently they delighted in making him suffer.

"Thanks," he said curtly.

Thankfully, they left him alone for his last hour at work. Al was beyond relieved: today had been more of an ordeal than he'd ever had at the wine shop. It wasn't taxing work, and usually he enjoyed the banter with customers; but today, with the constant erection pushing at his trousers, distracting his attention, making him *need* things he couldn't have...it had been horrendous. He was halfway out of the door before the final text came.

Come in, take off your clothes, and kneel by the sofa. L.

Laurie had timed it deliberately for the moment he left work. It left a strangely warm feeling in Al's chest that Laurie knew to the minute when he would be leaving the shop; he was angry with himself for getting so much pleasure from that thought, but at the same time it was very hot. The texts, he realised, showed that he'd been on Laurie and James's minds as much as they'd been on his. They wanted him. His cock throbbed hard at the thought.

When he got to the flat, there was no one in the sitting room. Obeying his instructions, he folded his clothes up and knelt naked by the empty sofa. Where were they? What were they doing? As Al got used to the sounds of the house, he realised that Laurie and James were in the kitchen. He could hear voices, and then the sloppy sounds of kisses. The noises got closer, and he glanced up to see that they were in the doorway between the sitting room and the kitchen, arms around each other, frotting up against one another as they kissed passionately. God, they were hot like that. And, Al realised, with frustrated fury, they knew he thought so. This was a show put on entirely for him...well, maybe not 'entirely'—James and Laurie were shamelessly obsessed with each other at any time—but the fact that they were simulating sex somewhere he could see them and not be part of it... They were deliberately teasing him, even more than they'd been doing all day. A frustrated growl burst from his lips.

James looked over, the faintest smile tracing his lips.

"Al's home," he told Laurie, as if it were a surprise.

"Mm-hm?" Laurie sounded supremely uninterested, going back to touching and snogging James as if there was nothing more he wanted from life.

And Al was going to bloody die if he didn't get any attention soon. His lovers were stripping each other's clothes off, kissing any part of each other which they could reach as they did so. James's mouth on Laurie's nipple, Laurie's head thrown back in pleasure, a hand behind James's head, encouraging him. James's hands busy on Laurie's trousers as he sucked, pushing them down, exposing Laurie's hard, heavy, large cock. They were distracted enough that they wouldn't notice if Al just had a quick touch. He couldn't bear it any longer. His left arm slid round from its required position behind him to take himself in hand, and he gave the tiniest hiss of relief at the sensation of fingers against his erection. Too quiet for anyone else to hear, you would have thought. Except that Laurie, with some psychic instinct, was suddenly gazing down at Al, a feral expression on his face.

"Oh, no, Al," he said, his voice dark and measured, his hand slipping from James's head. "That won't do at all. Did yesterday teach you nothing about obedience?"

James turned to look at him too, and Al swore under his breath. He was so, so fucked now.

"Please," he said pathetically, the word slipping out before he could prevent it. "God, please, Laurie. Please, Sir." He could hear the quiver in his voice and, clearly, so could Laurie.

Laurie's expression softened immediately. "Too much for you?" he asked, more gently. "You can just say your name, you know."

Al's name—his full name, Alistair—was his safeword. It was so very like Laurie to make sure he was reminded that he could use it at any time. But Al didn't want to—at least, he didn't think so. It was difficult to be certain of anything, feeling the way he did.

"No...yes... I don't know." Through a supreme effort of will, Al forced himself to put his hand back behind his back, clasping it firmly in his right. He'd got this damn close, got through the entire day and night. He couldn't lose it now. "I just..." A breath trembled out. "No, Sir," he managed.

"Well done," Laurie praised, lovingly.

He stepped out of his trousers and pants, coming over to sit on the sofa close to Al. So close. Al could feel the heat from Laurie's body, smell his arousal, and oh, bloody hell... Al squeezed his eyes closed and dug the fingers of one hand into the other. But frustratingly, his nails were chewed down to stubs, so there was no pinch of pain to distract him from his desire.

"Please. I just need—" Al wasn't sure what he needed, except for Laurie to let him come. Preferably to touch him, but at least let him touch himself. Let him have something before he died of sexual frustration.

"If I touch you, will you come?" Laurie asked.

James walked over to stand behind Al, placing warm hands on his shoulders and massaging them. The contact was both too much and not enough. It was James, and oh god, Al wanted James as much as he wanted Laurie. He made a little noise of frustration, leaning back into James's grasp.

"Yes," he whispered to Laurie, head bowed, embarrassed about his lack of control. "Probably, Sir."

Unexpectedly, Laurie leaned forward at this and touched his fingertips to Al's erection. It was electrifying; as if all the nerves in Al's body had flashed at once. Against his will, he cried out loudly, unable to stop himself from coming immediately, just at this tiniest of touches. His breath tore through his lungs, and he felt the frustratingly easy tears come to his eyes as his whole body trembled.

When he came back to himself, he realised he was speaking, crying out, "Oh god, oh god, oh god, oh god," over and over. He struggled to control his breathing, humiliated by his easy surrender and the fact that he had been unable to last more than that brief second. "I'm sorry," he said, as soon as he could, his head falling to Laurie's knee. "I'm sorry."

Laurie laughed, not unkindly, and stroked his hair, which had flopped around Al's face as he bent forward. "You don't think we've finished with you yet, do you, little slut? We've hardly more than begun."

"I... Oh god," Al said again.

"I've told you before," James said from behind him, "I'm good, but I'm not god." He laughed, low in his throat. "Neither is Laurie—quite."

"I couldn't help—"

"You've done nothing wrong," Laurie reassured him. "I asked, and you told me. You did everything right, our Al. It's okay. It's okay."

"I needed—"

"Yes. You did brilliantly, baby," Laurie said. "So good."

He pulled Al easily onto his lap, leaning back and holding him close. James came to sit next to them, putting one arm around each of them and pulling them both into a three-way hug. And Al felt loved, and looked after, and reassured beyond description. He made a small noise of contentment.

"I meant it, though," Laurie admonished, although his voice was fond. "I haven't finished with you, Al. Not by a long way. Neither James nor I have come yet tonight, which you are going to do something about in due course, and I expect you to come at least twice more before I'm done."

Al leaned in against Laurie's broad chest, his eyes closed. The fuzzy feeling engendered by orgasm and subspace combined, especially after the warm reassurance of his lovers, meant that it was hard for him to take in anything further which was said to him. He felt like he could rest here forever, safe and happy.

"I don't think he's listening to you, Laurie," James said, his tone amused.

"He will." The warmth was still there in Laurie's voice, but there was a slight edge of steel which pierced the edges of Al's consciousness.

"Yes, Sir," he said dozily, not really knowing what he was agreeing to; just willing to agree to anything Laurie told him.

"I was saying..." James said, laughingly.

Laurie made a noise of amusement in his chest which rumbled through Al's body. "He's allowed a moment. Don't worry. He'll be doing just as he's told in a minute, won't you, Al?"

Al was beginning to wake up to the fact that his lovers hadn't finished with him. Now that he'd had a few moments of recovery, he was getting some brain function returned to him.

"Yes, Sir. Anything," he said with a bit more attention.

"Good boy. See, James was massaging your shoulders just now, and I don't think that's the right way around. I think you need to be looking after James, don't you? Massaging him. Making *him* feel good. And whilst you're doing it, you can have a little think. Because James hasn't come yet, and maybe you can consider how you want to make him come; so after you've massaged him and looked after him a bit, you can beg for his cock the way you want it. You can rub his shoulders and decide whether you want his cock in your mouth or your arse, whether you want to touch him or just have him wank all over you; and then Jamie can make a decision on how good you've been and whether you get what you want or not. How does that sound, hmm?"

"God, a massage sounds lovely," James said, stretching. "I love my guitar, but I've taught so much today that I'm getting a cramp in my back. Thanks, Laurie."

"Don't thank me yet. See how well the slut can do and then decide if he's earned his reward." Laurie stood up, hoisting Al gently to his feet. There was no denying that Laurie's easy strength was one hell of a turn-on. "Bedroom, I think. Give you some space to lie down. I've got some massage oil somewhere, too."

It was no hardship to Al to massage a naked James's shoulders. He had a beautiful, muscular back, and Al sat astride him, smoothing oil into muscles and listening to the little noises of pain and pleasure James made when Al hit the right spots. His hands glided over the surface of James's warm skin, pressing firmly into knots where he found them. Laurie lay beside James, stroking his head and occasionally kissing him, as if there were moments when he just couldn't bear to keep from snogging his boyfriend. He spent most of the time, however, watching Al with stern but appreciative eyes as Al worked on James. And there was a heat in that gaze which sent tiny tremors through Al. It promised... It promised a lot, and all of it good.

Taking a quick look at Laurie from under his lashes, Al began to work his way further down James's back, sitting on James's arse and rocking gently as he did so. Already, the sensation of having his hands all over James's body was beginning to get Al in the mood for something more; and Laurie's hint about making him beg for James's cock was sending little tremors of anticipation through him. James really did have a beautiful cock. It was by no means as large as Laurie's—few people's, Al thought with happy appreciation, were—but it was long with a slight curve to it, and oh god, Al loved it. He adored sucking it, touching it, having James pound it into his arse. He realised he'd given a little sigh of pleasure at the thoughts going through his mind, which was a little embarrassing; getting off just on the very idea of James was perhaps a bit excessive. But then, he'd had a day of thinking of little else except for his boyfriends' many attributes and the wonderful ways they could use them. It was hardly his fault if they insisted on trying to drive him mad.

"Desperate again already? You really are such a cockslut, aren't you?" Laurie said, his voice a caress.

Al said the one thing he knew Laurie would understand. "James," he murmured. Laurie was as mad for James as Al was—more so, if that were possible.

Laurie laughed. "Well, yes," he acknowledged. He kissed James again. "So, gorgeous James, what do you think? Has he done enough to earn his reward?"

Al moved further down still, now using his hands to massage James's arse with long, smooth movements as he straddled his thighs. James gave a little moan.

"If he goes on doing things like that, I'm having him whether he wants me or not," he said.

Laurie laughed again. "I really don't think that's in doubt." His tone lowered. "I'd have you myself, if he hadn't done enough," he said, stroking a possessive hand down James's back and tucking it under his hip. "So bloody hot, laid out there like this, Jamie."

"I'm so bloody hard," James retorted.

Laurie raised an eyebrow at Al. "Well, little one, you've got some begging to do, haven't you?" He smirked. "That is, if you want James. I'm quite happy to see to my boyfriend's needs myself if you're not prepared to beg for it."

Half despite himself, Al made a little whining noise in his throat.

"No? You don't want me to do it for you?" Laurie asked. "On your knees, then."

Willingly, Al slid off the bed and onto his knees by the side of it, looking up pleadingly at James.

"Please, Jamie," he asked.

"What do you want?" James rolled onto his side, incidentally giving Al an extremely pleasurable view of his definitely hard cock, and smiled at Al.

Quite truthfully, Al hadn't actually got past the fact that he wanted James, and he wanted him now. James, oh god, James. He was honest. "I don't mind—I don't care. I just want you, James, please?"

"See what you do to people, Jamie?" Laurie said, his arms slipping around his lover from behind.

"The thing is, though," James said seriously to Al, "I have this amazing, hot boyfriend. And I'm not sure I'm willing to do anything that he's left out of. So we need to consider what you can possibly do for us both."

And Al's cock had gone from 'definitely interested in more' to 'really really want more right now' in about three seconds. If he'd do anything for James, and anything for Laurie...he'd do absolutely bloody everything for both of them together.

"Oh, please," he said fervently. "God, please, anything."

He sensed, rather than saw, the change of expression on Laurie's face at this; a tenderness and...could it really be surprise? Did Laurie seriously not know how much Al wanted him? Well, if he hadn't before, he certainly must now. Al was hardly being subtle. Even if his mouth hadn't given him away, his body would have done. Though Al's big mouth usually gave everything away, he thought ruefully. He never had been any good at shutting up, even at the best of times. Which this was.

It definitely was.

At least, as long as...

"Please, Sir," he added, raising his eyes to look at Laurie.

Laurie was capable of refusing him, even if he wanted him (or at least wanted James), if he thought that it was a lesson Al needed to learn. Al, however, felt that he had learned enough lessons about restraint for a while. He just wanted his lovers—his fucking amazing, sensual, sexual lovers. He tried to ignore the pulling, throbbing sensation in his groin as he thought about them. But there was silence from the bed, and Al was back to the place where he needed... He *needed*...

"Please, oh please," he found himself saying, resting his head against the edge of the bed. "James, god, I need..."

"You need to be fucked," James said, "and I'm intending to do it. But I know how good you are with your mouth around a cock, and I know how much you want Laurie. You do want to suck him off, don't you?"

"Yes, James," Al whispered. James wasn't a natural Dominant, not like Laurie. But it seemed he could have his moments, if only on grounds of fairness. It was just like James to be considering someone else's satisfaction at a moment when his own was supposed to be the subject at hand. It sent a sweet sense of warmth through Al.

"Why don't you get back on the bed, then?" James said; and it was a suggestion, not the order it would have been from Laurie. Nonetheless, it was one Al was very willing to comply with. "And you'd probably better ask Laurie nicely, if you want to get anywhere with him."

Al scrambled back onto the bed and onto his knees, putting his hands behind his back in his expected submissive posture, and dipping his head so that he was looking at the mattress. He could see his own cock, hard and bobbing between his legs as if it were doing some pleading of its own.

"Please, Sir," he said, "I want to suck your cock."

"Oh, do you?"

"Yes. Please."

"You really are such a cockslut, aren't you, Al?" Laurie asked, conversationally.

"Yes, Sir," Al said, willing to agree to anything if it got him what he wanted.

"Look at me," Laurie ordered, and Al obediently met his eyes. "You've already come all over yourself once. Think of the state of yourself, little slut, your come all up your belly and down your legs just because I touched you once—just because I put my fingers against your cock."

Al blushed. He was still a little humiliated about the immediacy of his reaction to Laurie's touch. "Yes, Sir," he mumbled, desperately wanting to look away from Laurie's gaze, but not daring to break the connection without permission.

"That's right. Look me in the eyes and know exactly what you are. And then I want to hear you say it," Laurie said ruthlessly.

"Sir?"

James had put a hand round Al's leg and was stroking his cock. It felt so good. Al wanted to press into the gentle grasp.

"I want to hear you admit that you're a shameless cockslut, just wanting to be filled and fucked," Laurie murmured, his voice warm and low. "I'm going to start to come in your mouth, and then I'm going to pull out and come all over you, make you look even more like the filthy slut you are. And you want that. You want to be covered in come. You want to feel Jamie's come sliding out of your arse as you drip with mine, don't you?"

"Yes, Sir." Oh god, yes.

"What are you, Al?"

James's hand was working faster on his cock, and Al could feel the press of James's erection against his hip. He was frightened that he'd moan the moment he opened his lips again, but Laurie was merciless, and Al knew he'd get nothing more out of Laurie or James until he answered.

"I'm—oh god—a cockslut, Sir."

"What?"

"Please—ohhh." The moan would out, with James rocking against him as his hand continued to move. Al could barely concentrate on anything, but Laurie wouldn't let him look away, wouldn't let him off the hook. He tried again, knowing he was begging, knowing that Laurie making him say this was making him harder than ever. "I'm a cockslut, I'm desperate for James to fuck me," Al said urgently. "Please, please, Jamie. Sir, I want to suck your cock. I want you in my mouth. Please. Oh god…"

Trying to hold on to the merest semblance of control was nearly impossible. There were tears in his eyes, and he didn't dare move his hands to dash them away. But it seemed that tonight, at least, he had done enough to earn his reward.

"God, you're hot," James muttered, taking his hand off Al's cock in order to flick open the lube and slather it onto himself. Al tried not to whine at the absence of James's touch.

"Isn't he?" Laurie agreed. "Good boy. Come and suck my cock, then, brat."

He shifted position to give Al access, and Al leaned forward, presenting his arse to James as he did so, his legs sliding apart. God, he wanted to be filled right now. His mouth closed around Laurie and he gave a little groan of thankfulness at the feeling, the taste. He loved the way Laurie tasted. James pressed against his arse, carefully opening him with his fingers before pushing his cock a little way inside. He paused, presumably waiting for Al to be ready for more, but Al was so very ready. Moaning, he pushed back against James, who sheathed himself inside his lover. And Al was being fucked at both ends, Laurie gently pushing into his mouth, whilst James just held himself deep inside Al for a few seconds. Al wasn't even being touched, but he was so damn horny, rocking back and forth in an attempt to get James to start moving. He slid his mouth off Laurie's cock, kissing his way up his boyfriend's erection and back down, before taking the shaft in one hand whilst his mouth and tongue worked over the head.

"Love you like this, Al," James said, thrusting into him.

Al could hear the slap of James's flesh against his own, taste Laurie's precome coating his tongue as he moaned again with the sensation. There was a musky, masculine smell of arousal which was turning Al's brain fuzzy with desire. Laurie's hand was on the back of his head, not forcing him forward but encouraging him to take more into his mouth, which Al was oh so willing to do. James was needier than usual, fucking him hard from the start, and it was as if Laurie was infected by James's eagerness. He was breathing heavily as Al sucked him, tilting his hips towards Al. Al couldn't speak with his mouth so thoroughly filled, but he knew he was making little pleading noises as he took his lovers' cocks inside him. James reached round to put his hand back on Al's erection, and Al whimpered, rutting back onto James's cock and forward into his hand, as his mouth still worked busily on Laurie. Laurie, he knew, was watching James take him hard; when Al's eyes flicked up, he could see the arousal in Laurie's face. Laurie had no desire to be fucked himself, but he loved watching James fuck Al—seeing his lover give out what he took from Laurie so often.

"James," Laurie said quietly, even though it was Al whose mouth was around his cock, and he was coming.

Al felt the first ejaculate hit his mouth, but then, as he'd promised, Laurie pulled out, painting Al's face and neck and chest with warm, white threads of come. Al could feel it sliding over his skin—dirty and wrong and so fucking hot. His hands grasped helplessly at Laurie's legs as he cried out loudly and came in turn.

"Beautiful slut," Laurie said warmly, sliding down and kissing Al even as he rode out his orgasm.

James moved with longer strokes now, holding Al's hips hard and withdrawing almost completely before thrusting back in with purpose. Al was only being kept up by the force of Laurie's grip under his arms, of James's on his hips. He felt boneless, just there to be used by James...and he loved it. Laurie had once teasingly asked him if he wanted to be James's fucktoy, and just now Al felt like that was precisely what he was. Nothing but what James made him.

"James, Jamie, please," he heard himself pleading.

"Yes. Fuck."

James gave a long groan and at last reached his own completion, driving into Al one last time and staying there, shuddering, as his orgasm took him. James's grip loosened on Al's hips, and the two of them slid to the bed, James lying heavily across Al's legs and back. Laurie lowered Al's front so that his head was resting on Laurie's shoulder, the three of them a mass of bodies with Al sandwiched between his two lovers.

"There, now," Laurie said, a teasing note in his voice as he wrapped his arms all the way around Al and rested them on James's shoulders. "That's much better, isn't it?"

"Yes, Sir," Al said instinctively, not even sure whether Laurie was speaking to him or not.

Laurie ruffled his hair. "It's okay, baby. Just lie there."

Al snuggled into the side of Laurie. When he was submissive, he needed to be close to his boyfriends after sex. It took him a while to recover his equanimity, and until he did, he was in need of physical reassurance in a way which bore no resemblance to his everyday self. But both partners knew it and were always careful to look after him at such times. Al sometimes wondered, later, where the confident version of himself had gone—and yet, he knew it took much more confidence, both in himself and in his partners, to be able to let go to that extent. To give absolutely everything of himself to his lovers and trust them to take care of him. He breathed in Laurie's scent and relished the weight of James's body across his own, grounding him. Bringing him back.

Laurie kept his word, however, and Al came once more before the evening was out, this time with Laurie's mouth around his cock, James's mouth against his own. By the time he went to sleep that evening, Al had to admit that he was perhaps more sexually satisfied than he'd ever been in his life, and that maybe, although he still maintained that his boyfriends were evil sexual sadists for making him wait, just maybe they might have been on to something. God, he felt good. Al stretched heavy limbs, knowing he would be able to feel the after-effects in the morning. He revelled in the thought, and fell asleep listening to the quiet sounds of Laurie's breathing beside him whilst the soft notes of James's guitar filtered through the door from the sitting room. He was happy.

Chapter Two

JAMES

It was a Tuesday evening. James strummed a few chords quietly, his fingers moving up and down the guitar by instinct more than conscious thought. Laurie was sitting on the sofa, glancing at his phone, Al leaning against him as he worked on his laptop—probably organising the details of his next film.

They looked comfortable. James still found it kind of odd, watching his boyfriends cuddled up with each other. Sex—he had no issues with watching them have sex. That seemed normal enough—which, James supposed, said a lot about the weirdness both of his mind and their relationship in itself. But it was the *homeliness* of this sort of interaction which seemed...well, disconcerting. He didn't mind—certainly not in a negative way. In fact, it was rather sweet. (James suppressed a grin: both men, and Al in particular, would want to throttle him if they knew he was assessing them as 'sweet'). But it was nonetheless distinctly peculiar. Al snuggling with anyone in a non-sexual sort of fashion seemed hugely unlikely, and yet he looked so content pressed up against Laurie's side, concentrating hard on whatever it was he was examining on his computer. James segued into "Brown Eyed Girl" by Van Morrison and thought about the fact that his life was pretty much perfect.

"Oh," said Laurie, a slight note of strain in his voice cutting over James's thoughts about perfection.

"What?" Absently, James continued to play, even as he looked over at Laurie.

"Gillie wants to know if I'm avoiding her."

Gillie. James's mother, and incidentally Laurie's best friend. Oh, and just to make matters even more complicated, she considered Al as good as another son, as well.

"Are you?" asked Al, leaning back a little further on his partner's lap and looking up at Laurie with interest.

Laurie glared back down at him irritably. "Of course I bloody am. Have been for...oh, about seven weeks or so?"

Seven weeks. Had it really only been seven weeks since the three of them 'officially' became a triad? Their lives had been so complicatedly bound up together for so long that it was difficult to work out where one stage had ended and another begun. Sometimes James wondered how they hadn't realised it would end up like this. At other times, he still couldn't believe that Al was voluntarily—*very* voluntarily—in an actual relationship. Nor that James and Laurie had found enough room in their love for another person. One thing that James could say for certain was that it wasn't because Laurie wasn't enough for him. Laurie was everything. It was just...so was Al.

The trouble was, how to say any of this to James's mum. She loved them all dearly and had been very supportive of James and Laurie's relationship—but that didn't necessarily mean that she was precisely going to approve of the fact that they were now a polyamorous threesome. James knew that Laurie had felt peculiar enough keeping from her the fact that he and James slept with Al on a fairly regular basis, which had been the case for a couple of years now. However, Laurie had agreed that this was not something that James's mother necessarily needed to know about, to James's great relief. Now that they were properly together, though... James had a nasty feeling he knew where Laurie's train of thought was going, and it was somewhere that James really didn't want it to.

He was right.

"I have to tell Gillie," Laurie said. James had heard Laurie sound happier, too.

"So tell her." Al snapped down the lid of his laptop and pushed it onto the table.

"Do we really have to tell her?" James countered.

He found his heart beating faster every time he considered explaining to his mother that yes, he was indeed fucking two blokes, even if those two blokes were Laurie and Al. Some things, you really didn't want to share with your mother.

"She's my best friend, James," Laurie said, pleadingly. "I can't keep—well, pretty much *lying* to her, can I? You know damn well you'd tell your best friend."

Al and James—best friends for fifteen years and more—caught each other's eye and they both sniggered. "Erm," James said, unable to repress a grin, "I'm pretty sure he already knows."

Laurie made a little irritated noise in his throat. "Were it not," he said grimly, "for the fact that you were bloody sleeping with him. Christ, what the fuck am I going to tell her? 'Oh, hi, Gillie. Why, yes, I have been avoiding you just a bit. And by the way, did you know I'm two-timing your son with his best friend?'"

James decided that Al had had the right idea when he'd closed his laptop. He put his guitar to one side and joined the other two on the sofa.

"You're not exactly two-timing me," he pointed out, kissing Laurie lightly on the lips. (It was impossible to be this close to Laurie and not kiss him. That was simple fact.) His lips tingled pleasurably, even as he tried to concentrate on the matter at hand. "I think I'm fairly aware of your intentions towards Al."

"Mm," agreed Al, running a hand down Laurie's leg and simultaneously reaching out to pull James closer with the other arm. "So am I. Dishonourable all the way, I hope."

"Hey," James objected, falling into his age-old pattern of conversation with Al, "he was living in sin with me first."

Al grinned, a glint in his eye. "I've just upped the sin quotient," he retorted.

"Yes, you...well, no," Laurie said, sighing and dropping a kiss onto the top of Al's head. "No, you haven't. I mean, it...it's not like..."

He cut off, as Al began to kiss James, pulling him hard in against him and licking over the contours of his lips before gently persuading James to open his mouth. James moaned, just a little. Al was one hell of a kisser. And a hell of a distraction. But after a short time, he pulled away.

"Sin quotient duly upped," James acknowledged, his mouth tingling further, and a warm heat pooling in his groin. "The problem is Mum."

"She's not a problem," Laurie said quickly, defensively. "I just...don't think she's going to be particularly thrilled."

"Blimey," said Al mournfully, "and I thought she liked me."

James gave him a shove at this comment. "She does, you dick. It's just..."

"She may think that it's not exactly...appropriate for me to be sleeping with the pair of you." Laurie groaned and tugged at his hair. "In fact, she might actually kill me."

"Leave your hair alone." James gently reached over and disentangled Laurie's hand from its grasp of his head, then clasped it in his own. "Anyway, I don't know why you think it's you she's going to be furious with. Al and I have a bit to do with things as well."

"Also, she's quite keen on you both," Al pointed out briskly. "And it's not like we're committing a criminal offence or anything. Gillie's cool."

Laurie took a deep breath. "Yes. Yeah, you're right." He didn't sound wildly convinced, but he was clearly doing his best. "Okay, I'll tell her."

"*We'll* tell her," James corrected him. He gave Al a firm look, and Al smiled and rolled his eyes, which James knew was acceptance. "There are three of us in this relationship. We can all take responsibility."

Thus it was that the following Sunday, James, Laurie, and Al descended onto James's mother's house. Laurie had texted, asking if they could visit, and got the immediate response *Of course. Delighted! Come to tea!* So here they were. James took a deep breath and rang the doorbell.

"Hey, Mum." James gave his mother a hug on the doorstep as the other two said their hellos over his shoulder.

"Hello, darlings!" Gillie's arms surrounded her son, but her smile embraced all three of them. "My son, my adopted son, and my best friend. It's so good to see all of you together."

"To be fair, we do live in the same house," Al pointed out. "We're together quite a lot."

She gave him a mock-severe glare. "Yes, but you don't all come to visit me, do you? In fact, young man, when was the last time you were here at all?"

Al had the grace to look embarrassed, James was amused to note. "A while back? Didn't think you particularly wanted to see me—haven't you had enough of me by now?"

She reached up and ruffled his hair. "Never enough of you, Al, as you should know perfectly well by now. Anyway, come in. To what do I owe this honour?"

"We really came to talk to you about something," Laurie admitted.

"Oh?" Gillie glanced between the three of them. "Should I be concerned? Do I need to sit down?"

"Why don't we all sit down?" Laurie suggested.

"Now that," Al said, "sounds like a brilliant idea."

Gillie ushered them into the sitting room, where the three men sat on the sofa and she ensconced herself on a chair, her enormous ginger cat Roger leaping immediately into her lap the moment she sat down. He really did have the loudest purr, James thought, not for the first time. And apparently he wasn't alone in being distracted by the cat.

"Is he really a tiger?" Al asked absently, watching Gillie stroke the big beast.

"Al," Gillie scolded, "are you trying to change the subject?"

James had sort of wondered that himself. Though it wasn't like Al. Hell, Al had been the only one out of the three of them who hadn't been freaking out about this conversation.

"Oh. Sorry," Al apologised. "God, he's a monster, though, isn't he? Aren't you, Roger-beastie?"

Though Al wouldn't admit it, James knew that Al was rather attached to cats. He couldn't help feeling that Al would have made rather a good cat himself. Nonetheless, this was hardly the time to start chatting about felines, given the awkward conversation that they'd actually come to have with James's mother. Now that they were actually here, James just wanted to get it over with—though he still didn't have the faintest idea how to start telling her about them. When he and Laurie had got together, his mum had had some idea that it was coming—or at least that something was. Laurie had, after all, just admitted to her that he had been fantasising about James for years. James, accidentally overhearing this, had barged in demanding what the hell Laurie was talking about, and James's mum had made a tactful disappearance. Their later reappearance together, holding hands, had said it all for them. James had never had to say a word about his relationship. But as far as he knew, his mother still didn't know he'd ever slept with Al, whether recently or in the pre-Laurie past.

"Al, shut up about the cat," James suggested, politely. "We didn't come to talk about Roger."

"Not this time," added Laurie, with a quick smile.

"Come on then," Gillie said, "out with it—whatever 'it' may be." She smiled. "I don't imagine it can be that bad, since you all three appear to be talking to each other."

"Oh yes," said Laurie, his voice becoming a little hollow. "We're definitely talking to each other. In fact..."

"The thing is—" said James, and broke off, unsure how to phrase it.

"We're a—" It was Laurie's turn to break off.

"Threesome," Al added helpfully. James looked at him gratefully, and saw that Laurie was doing the same thing. The look of gratitude faded, however, as Al added, "Which means we're having—"

"Al!" The warning came from both Laurie and James, and Al looked innocently back at them, before turning back to Gillie.

"A relationship," he said calmly.

James seethed quietly, knowing that Al had not been able to resist the temptation to wind the other two up. Both James and Laurie had been in a state of angst about this conversation for days. If James was worried about how his mother would take tales of his complicated love life, Laurie was positively terrified. James's mother was his best friend, and James knew that Laurie wasn't sure whether fucking both her son and her unofficial adopted son would be beyond the reaches of any friendship. Laurie had been concerned, originally, about how Gillie would feel about him being with just James; it had almost been enough to stop their relationship before it even started. He was therefore petrified that adding Al—whom Gillie also loved as a son—to the mix would be a deal-breaker. James couldn't really believe that his mum would turn on Laurie...but Laurie's doubts had infected him, making him even more nervous than he'd been before. Because, frankly, informing your mother you were dating two people was never going to be the easiest of conversations. James's parents had had a nice, sensible, heterosexual, monogamous relationship until the day his dad died. And whilst James knew his mother didn't give a damn about the fact that he was gay, he couldn't help feeling that she maybe didn't need to know that he was also apparently polyamorous. Al had been the only calm one in the flat for a while, and James knew that his best friend—his, well, bloody hell, his other *boyfriend*—had been coping as patiently as he could with the other two. This, no doubt, was his gentle revenge. James supposed he should be grateful it wasn't worse.

Gillie was sitting quite still. James had seen her blink several times in quick succession, but apart from that, she was showing no signs of what she was thinking. Her hand stilled on Roger's back, and he stood up and turned around disconsolately, in comparison showing his displeasure quite clearly before settling down again.

"Can you run that past me again, please?" she said slowly.

She looked between the three of them, her gaze lingering longest on Laurie, her best friend. Her son's lover, now outed as Al's lover, too. Maybe, James thought anxiously, she just couldn't even bear the thought of Al and James together. She called Al her 'other son'—surely she wouldn't see their relationship as incestuous? They weren't related, after all, despite a vague similarity in looks which had meant that they'd regularly been mistaken for brothers in the past. They'd been close friends for years; and yes, this was something very different from a normal friendship, but...they were still themselves, James and Al, just as they had always been. Had they really done something unforgivable, something even James's own mother couldn't forgive them for? James had a much closer relationship with his mother than most twenty-five-year-old men, he knew. He hated the thought of being alienated from her.

"Um..." James said.

James looked at his mother and then at Laurie and Al, pleadingly. Laurie looked as if he feared Gillie was going to hit him. James knew he probably ought to say something—it was his mother, after all—but he just couldn't. Al opened his mouth to repeat the information he'd just given (presumably, though one never knew with Al), but Laurie unexpectedly beat him to it, perhaps fearing what Al might say next.

"James and Al and I are together," he said steadily. "All three of us."

He still looked like he expected a punch from Gillie; whether physical or verbal, James couldn't tell. James, however, could feel his mother's eyes right on him, no one else. Fuck, he wished he had some idea what she was thinking. His heart gave an uncomfortable thump.

"James?"

"You're not going to disown me, are you, Mum?" James asked. He was trying to make a joke out of it, but there was an element of seriousness in his question, and he had a horrible feeling it was fairly obvious to them all.

Gillie sighed and leaned back, her eyes scanning all three of them. "Are you all happy?" she asked.

Oh, Mum. *That* was her concern—that whilst two of them might be happy about this new dynamic, the third might not? Not that there was something intrinsically wrong in it, but that someone she loved might be hurt. God, his mother was brilliant. James thought about his boyfriends' mothers: Laurie's had seen him as a disappointment, right up until her death; Al's had... Al had once said that she'd told him that he'd ruined her life. James still couldn't quite believe any parent would say something precisely that blunt, but it was true that Al's parents had moved to America, making it clear they had little interest in seeing their only son. It was also true that James's mum had mothered Al much more than Al's own mother ever had. James was so bloody lucky.

"I'm all right," Al assured her.

"Very much so," Laurie said, putting an arm around each of his boyfriends.

James leaned into the touch, resting his head against Laurie's shoulder. There was something about Laurie touching him, still, which prompted an almost instinctive need to touch back. James had been in love with Laurie for so many years before they'd got together. Even now, three and a bit years into their relationship, he still sometimes had trouble believing that his boyfriend could really want him. Warmth flowed through him from everywhere Laurie's body touched his own. James loved Al to bits, and couldn't even begin to imagine living without him, but Laurie was...Laurie.

"I do believe I'll manage," James said. He looked at his mother with dancing eyes, a smile beginning to form. He had Laurie. He had Al. He had a mother in a million—in a billion.

There was a puff of relief from Gillie, and a smile slid over her face in turn. "Then I am delighted for you, my dears," she said. With a clear effort, she forced the smile from her face, however. "But what*ever* will the neighbours think?" she asked; and they all laughed.

Chapter Three

AL

It was amazing what a change there had been in the flat over the last couple of months, since they'd all finally come out to James's mother about the fact that they were a triad. Christmas was over and done with, during which time all of them had descended on Gillie to celebrate the festive period. The best thing—the best Christmas present Al could have got, in fact—was how clear it had been when they were there that Gillie truly didn't mind the fact that all three of them were together. Fortunate, really, thought Al, amused, considering the amount they all touched. They weren't exactly a subtle bunch when it came to physical demonstrations of their feelings for one another. If Gillie had been in a mood to complain, she'd have had a hell of a time. And so would the rest of them.

Gillie was not just James's parent—James, therefore, would presumably have done okay, whatever happened; apparently decent parents didn't disown their only kids (Al wouldn't know; his pretty much had)—but she was also Laurie's best friend.

Al remembered the days when he was just a child and Laurie was a Proper Grown-Up of whom he'd been slightly in awe, though he would never have admitted it. Laurie had been at university when Al first knew him, doing film studies. As a ten-year-old, Al had thought it was the most incredible thing anyone could possibly learn about—and he hadn't changed his mind. Rather to his private mortification, eight years later he'd ended up doing exactly the same course as Laurie had, at the very same university...and worse, with Laurie newly working there as a sessional lecturer. Al had never acknowledged out loud how self-conscious that had made him; he hoped that no one, not even Laurie or James (hell, especially them!), had ever realised. On the other hand, he'd only known Laurie because of Gillie, James's mother.

And Gillie was... Al didn't know how to describe what Gillie was to him. It felt...a little bit frightening when he thought about it. Because Gillie had always been there. Not like she was for Laurie—the whole best friend thing. Not exactly as she was for James, either—but partly because Al couldn't relax, couldn't bring himself to trust a parent-figure, not after his own experiences. If he had been going to reach out to someone in that way, though, there would only be one person he'd turn to. "My adopted son" Gillie called him, and Al wanted, sometimes painfully much, for that to be true. He was good at covering it, though, treating Gillie with an easy, loving familiarity. Al hadn't been able to admit it, not with the state both James and Laurie had been in, but he too had been worried about how Gillie would take the news of their relationship. She'd have loved James whatever. Of course she would. And Al was pretty sure that Gillie would forgive Laurie most things. But despite his bravado, Al had been terrified that Gillie would hate him for coming between Laurie and James, who had been a devoted couple for years. They were the happy couple. He was the interloper, and he'd wondered whether that was what Gillie would see: that Al had taken her son and best friend's perfect relationship and marred it.

Especially because, much as he loved his boyfriends, Al wasn't sexually faithful to them. James and Laurie knew, and understood, that this was the case. Gillie...probably didn't. She knew, Al knew, that Al had a promiscuous past; whether she was aware that he also had a promiscuous present, James and Laurie notwithstanding, was less clear. It was unlikely; the words "in a relationship" tended to imply exclusivity. His only consolation was that his partners—not just James and Laurie, but all of the others—certainly did know where they stood.

Which was why, on this braw January evening, James wandered in from the kitchen, as Al got ready to leave the house, and said casually, "Oh, what? Going out to get laid tonight, by any chance?"

"Yep," Al replied, smiling. "With any luck, at any rate. Got a date with a hot blonde."

"Male or female?" James asked, looking interested.

Al laughed. "Female. Sorry, mate."

James rolled his eyes. "I'm taken, anyway. Some of us find two boyfriends enough, you know."

"Don't start boasting about that," Al advised, with a grin. "A lot of people might suggest that's one too many as it is. And yes, before you tell me, I realise I'm the 'one too many', but you're the one who invited me into bed with you and Laurie."

"One moment," James said, raising his hands as in disbelief. "One moment, and it gets thrown back at me forever. How the fuck did I know I'd end up living with you? It was supposed to be a one-off, and stop Laurie smoking into the bargain—"

"Well, at least it worked for that," Al pointed out.

"And now I'm stuck with you forever more, apparently," James finished, ignoring the interjection.

Al moved up close to James and put his arms around him, resting his hands firmly on his boyfriend's arse. "I'd make you admit you love every minute," he murmured, "but I've got a hot date to go on." He stood on tiptoe to align their bodies—he was several inches shorter than James— and then ground up against his lover, who rolled his hips back in response, with no shame. "Hold that thought."

"I'll hold that thought—and myself—to my other bloody boyfriend, who isn't off doing weird things with women," James grumbled; but Al grinned as he kissed him and stepped away.

The lovely thing about his partners was that they had not even the smallest problem with him dating other people. They knew that it made no difference to his love for them. And Al did love them, beyond anything he'd ever believed himself capable of. But for him, sex was like friendship. You wouldn't ask someone to have no other friends, just because you were their closest friend. Sex, like friendship, could take place on many different levels and be enjoyable just for what it was. Al didn't sleep with people he didn't like; but just as someone else might spend an interesting evening chatting to a stranger in a pub, Al might spend one in bed with that same stranger. As long as everyone involved understood the basis on which the interaction was taking part, there could be no harm done. And Al would never, ever, have sex with anyone who didn't go along with his morals (and his standards—protection was obligatory with anyone who wasn't James or Laurie). They weren't for everyone, that was true—but it was surprising how many people were quite fine with it, so long as everything was honest and above board. Which was, conveniently, just the way Al liked it. He had James and Laurie, his loves. He also had two or three other people whom he saw on a regular or semi-regular basis—Gemma, a backing singer in a prestigious pop group, being top of these.

Gemma was probably his best friend aside from his boyfriends—she'd met Laurie and James on several occasions, and they got on well. Like Al, Gemma had plenty of other partners—all male; she was decidedly straight—but the two of them had a close friendship, and were extremely sexually compatible. Al was always glad to see her. However, Gemma wasn't his date tonight. Tonight, Al was seeing a new lady—one who had flirted heavily with him on a night out the previous week. She'd seemed to know something of his reputation and, as always, Al had made it clear that he was not in the market for a relationship, something Brooke had seemed perfectly happy to hear.

"Well, babe," she had said sweetly, "if it's to be one night, let it be a night to remember."

Al had agreed and had been very much looking forward to the evening. However, halfway through the date, he was beginning to think that for once he'd made a mistake. Brooke was so very...entitled. She'd spent most of the evening talking about the things her daddy—the owner (not the editor, the *owner*: a difference she seemed determined to be clear about) of a fairly big London-centric newspaper, for which she worked—had bought her. Al zoned out, he hoped subtly, and started gazing around at the other people in the restaurant. There were a middle-aged couple having a quiet but heated row and a family trying to keep their children in check, while over to his left sat two young men snogging like the rest of the world didn't exist. Al couldn't help a small smile at that last. When he returned his attention to Brooke, she was still talking about her newspaper job; she seemed, in fact, to have few conversations save about herself. Still, she seemed otherwise pleasant enough, and she was definitely attractive—and very into Al, judging by the way she had invited him back to her place and was now kissing him with little reservation. In fact, he told himself, it would probably all be fine. Maybe she was nervous. Nervous but nice—that was probably it.

Famous last words.

It was at that point, Brooke said, her high-pitched voice clear and malicious, "Gosh, did you see those awful fags kissing in the restaurant? It was almost enough to put me off my dinner."

"I beg your pardon?" said Al, startled.

Her eyes widened dramatically. "Oh, wasn't I politically correct there? You know, gays. Didn't you see them? I wouldn't mind so much if they kept it to themselves, but in *public*... Don't you think? I know"—

she batted her eyelashes at him—"*real* men don't like that sort of thing. I mean, personally I don't hate gay people, but you have to admit what they do in the bedroom is revolting. Sticking their you-know-what where. I don't even want to think about it. It's practically bestiality."

Al had been silent from shock for a few seconds. He had thought that his own proclivities were fairly well stated, and so would have suspected Brooke of winding him up had she not made it extremely clear over the rest of the evening that she didn't have a sense of humour. Damping down on the temptation to start yelling at her and telling her his unvarnished opinion of homophobes in reply, he instead leaned forward.

"Oh, do tell me more," he purred seductively. "I love it when people talk dirty to me." He gave her a little, wicked smile. "Tell me some more about these men and what they're doing with their dicks."

"I...what?" Brooke was almost squeaking in indignation.

"Come on," Al murmured, "you know you find it hot. Why else would you bring it up?"

There was an evil pleasure in watching the expressions cross his definitely-not-going-to-be-a sex-partner's face.

"I—I don't! I—"

Brooke was incoherent with her rage. It made Al all the more coolly voluble. He looked her straight in the eyes.

"As you say, I'm extremely keen on girls," he acknowledged. "But maybe before you start mouthing off about gay sex, you might consider making sure you're not talking to someone who's shacked up with two other men, yeah?" Her mouth fell open. "Oh yes," Al confirmed, a tiny smile gracing his lips. "In fact, if you'll excuse me, I think I might go home and see if I can persuade my fit, strapping boyfriend to put his you-know-what in my you-know-where and fuck me so hard I scream."

"You're revolting."

"If I'm really lucky, my other gorgeous boyfriend might even let me rim him," Al continued, on a roll now. He stood up, pushing away from his chair, still looking at Brooke. She didn't look quite so gorgeous with her face curled up in disgust. "That tongue that's been in your mouth tonight, 'babe'? It's been so far up another man's arse, it's amazing you couldn't taste it." His smile became broader. "And I loved every single second of it. Night, Brooke."

He walked out, aware of her staring after him the whole way. Maybe he'd gone too far, but fucking hell. He hadn't spoken to someone quite that openly homophobic for some time, and his mouth had run away with him. He grinned a little, remembering her expression, and walked home. Laurie was home now, and he and James were on the sofa—not having sex, for once, but watching a film while Laurie talked James through the different tricks which were being used in the cinematography, in preparation for a class on the morrow.

"Hey," said James, looking up and pausing the film. "You're back early."

"Mm." Al pulled a face.

"Did it not go well? I thought you had a hot date."

"Ugh." Al slumped to the floor in front of the sofa, leaning against it. "Yeah, great date until she started telling me how disgusting queers were. It kind of went downhill from there."

"Tactless," Laurie said. "Didn't she know?"

"Apparently not. She does now," Al added coldly. "In detail. I think she regretted snogging me when I told her everywhere my tongue had been."

"Bloody hell, Al," James said, half laughing, "you didn't?"

Al leaned his head back against James's knee. "Pretty much. I probably shouldn't have said it, but I kind of lost it for a moment. Told her I was going home to get my fit boyfriends to fuck me stupid, if I could stop rimming you for more than three seconds. Or something along those lines, anyway."

The other two both snorted at this, but Laurie shook his head. "You're better than that, Al."

"Oh, I don't know. He's quite good at that," James said, grinning.

Laurie prodded him. "Not rimming, you idiot. You know what I mean. No need to descend to someone else's level. Though very tempting."

"Comparisons between gay sex and bestiality tend to piss me off," Al said grimly.

"What the...? Seriously?" James's eyes were flashing with anger. "To be honest, Laurie, I think he was fairly mild in his reaction."

"Well, I wasn't exactly going to punch her, was I?" Al retorted. "But I couldn't let it go, Laur."

Laurie sighed. "No, I don't think I could have done, either—though it's not the first time I've heard that comparison made. You two make me feel old, sometimes; a decade might not seem like much, but thank god people tend to be a bit more restrained about what they say than they were when I first came out."

"Trust me, our school was not a hotbed of tolerance," Al assured him. "We've heard most things—me, particularly. Jamie was sensible enough not to mention his proclivities, which is something I wasn't very good at."

"Still aren't, judging by this evening," James murmured.

"Yeah, well. I think there's someone I won't be seeing again; put it that way," Al said. "Come on, Laurie, stick the film back on and tell me all about it. It's been a while since I've been in one of your lectures."

The rest of the evening passed well, and by the time Al went to bed, he had calmed down. Sure, Brooke was a homophobic idiot, but it happened. They'd made their views quite clear to one another, and there was no need for him to see her ever again. It was fine.

By the time a fortnight had passed, he'd pretty much forgotten about her.

BUT IF AL had thought that was the end of things, he couldn't have been more wrong. Working at home on a new film project a few weeks later, Al looked up as James got back from the music school he worked at. He flashed him a smile, but found himself stopped in his tracks by the expression on his boyfriend's face. Al's smile faded.

"Jamie, what's the matter?" he asked urgently, pushing himself out of his seat.

"Al. I..." James stopped, swallowed. "Someone at work gave me this," he said briefly, holding out a newspaper.

Mystified, Al took the paper from James's shaking hand, looking down at it. It was folded open at an inside page, and Al found himself faced by a picture of himself. Not entirely unusual; his film-making meant he was occasionally featured in papers, though he still honestly found it a bit peculiar. However, there were two ominous factors—apart from James's expression—about this particular occasion. One was the fact that there was a small photo, inset, of Laurie. The other was the headline.

"Oh god," said Al, nervously, and started to read.

It wasn't as bad as he feared. It was much, much worse.

Al-together Sick: Film-maker's Sordid Sex Romps

His film Welding the Night Away, *updating the theme of the madwoman in the attic to a garage in London, scored critical success. His current project, a story about a mother's struggle with gender confusion, looks set to do better still. But perhaps it is director Al Hitchins's own life which is the most lurid of all—too shocking even for the big screen.*

At another point, Al might have been furious about this appalling take on his films. To call Helen, the main character in *Welding*, a 'madwoman' was not only offensive but completely missed the point of her incredible strength and bravery while dealing with mental illness; whilst anyone less confused about his gender than Jack, the trans man central character in *Transparent* was hard to imagine. But he had a horrible feeling that James hadn't given this to him for the sake of the paper's libel of his film-making.

He read on.

Al Hitchins flaunts the fact he lives with, and is in a sexual relationship with, two other men simultaneously—James Cape and Dr Laurence Rose. Cape, a man Hitchins's own age, who is a childhood friend, is a shop worker.

What the hell? Al was open about the fact he slept around, but as far as he'd known up to this point, his relationship with James and Laurie specifically was a private matter. Gemma, his long-term sort-of-girlfriend knew about them and had met them—but she wouldn't have told anyone, and she certainly wouldn't have claimed he was flaunting the relationship. The whole thing was simply bizarre.

Bizarre...and, it seemed, much worse than just bizarre.

Dr Rose, a much older man, is a lecturer at the Metropolitan University of West and North London. It is not clear precisely how long Dr Rose has officially been in a relationship with the young men; however, he has known them intimately since they were ten years old and he more than twice their age. To date one much younger partner might be chance; when it comes to bedding two of them, it suggests a fetish—or worse. Whether this makes Rose the sort of man appropriate to teach naïve eighteen-year-olds—and what he may be teaching them—is open to opinion. It should be noted that Dr Rose was one of Hitchins's lecturers during his time at the university.

"Laurie's going to kill me." Al looked up at James when he reached this point, hoping for reassurance that he didn't get. "Shit," he said.

James was still standing, pale and clammy-looking, watching Al read the article. He had said nothing since handing it to Al—a forbearance which was much more concerning than any number of furious criticisms would have been.

Other lines leapt out at Al:

As to Hitchins himself, you might think that two partners would be— well, more than enough; but apparently the sex-mad director doesn't agree. Preying predominantly on women, it seems that Hitchins is on a mission to get as many notches as possible on his bedpost, whether his chosen partners like it or not. Regulars in certain local pubs say that Hitchins has been seen with as many as a dozen different 'conquests' in the course of a month.

At another time, Al might have laughed at that last line. Even in the days he'd been interested in no-strings sex most nights, just for the sheer pleasure of it (and there had been pleasure—lots of it, for his partners as well as himself, Al both hoped and believed), he should have been so lucky. Recently, what with James and Laurie, and his long-term casual hook-ups, he rarely slept with anyone new more than once a month—if that—and had no urge for more. Plus, as many of his partners were male as female; but that was kind of a side issue, in the circumstances. The word 'preying', however, rarely preceded any positive sort of comment.

Whether the unfortunate ladies have the experience they are hoping for is another matter, however. Whilst his perverted tastes mean that few women are prepared to speak about their experiences, one woman described a scene with the 'gentleman'. She told us, "He was kissing me, and then he stopped and said, 'I've just had my tongue so far up a man's arse I'm surprised you can't taste it.' I felt violated." She refused to say more, and it is impossible to say how far his violations may go, or how many women may have suffered at his hands.

Oh. Oh fuck. That sounded horribly familiar. Al's eyes slid back up to the top of the paper, where he read the name of the journalist. Brooke Lingarten. The entitled daddy's girl whose father...oh yes, owned this particular paper. Quoting herself as an independent witness. How very professional. And the hint that he'd done more to her than just insulted her was perfectly phrased, making it impossible to deny without seeming to prove it in so doing. She refused to say more? Of course she did; there was nothing more to say. But that didn't matter. The damage was already done.

He scanned the rest of the article. There was not much more, just a couple of lines.

The quality, or otherwise, of Al Hitchins's films may be a matter of taste. They aren't to mine. But his personal life can only be seen at best as tasteless, and at worst, depraved.

Al looked suddenly at James. "Someone at your work gave you this?" he asked.

James nodded.

"For...this?"

"Yeah."

"Fuck."

Al had hoped that James, at least, might be fairly anonymous. His name was hardly that unusual, and Brooke's desire to degrade James from music teacher to shop worker made the description of him less than obvious.

"They recognised Laurie."

Oh, bloody hell, of course they would. Laurie and James had been dating for over three-and-a-half years. Laurie had been down to the music school every now and then in that time. Of course he had. And with a picture as well as the description in the paper? Hardly subtle. Al cursed silently. He wanted to ask about the spirit in which the paper had been handed over, but he wasn't sure he dared. It was one thing being out as gay—though James had been much more cautious even about that than Al had been about his own sexuality. James had known since he was fourteen that he was gay, confided in Al at fifteen, and not come out publicly until he left school at eighteen. Al, meanwhile, had discovered his bisexuality at seventeen and been open about it from the beginning. Though he had to admit that without James's support, his final year at school might have been considerably more traumatic. That, he thought suddenly, could describe his life, however—James's loyalty and friendship had helped him through a number of bad times, including an unexpected and very un-Al-like bout of depression when they'd been sixteen. Al had barely recognised himself during the worst of those days, but James had pulled him through, willing to sit with him for hours to make sure he was safe as Al talked quite genuinely about killing himself. Al bit his lip. This was how he repaid James's friendship? By involuntarily outing James as part of a polyamorous relationship—and with two people who had more or less been described as an abusive sex fiend (Al) and potential paedophile (Laurie). It would hardly be anyone's first choice of scenario, let alone a private person such as James.

"Sorry." Al suspected it would not be the last time he uttered that word. If only he could demonstrate how sincerely he meant it.

"Not your fault," James said shortly.

Al flushed. "It is, though. Not just for being..." He flicked the paper dismissively. "Well, I'm none of this crap, but I am promiscuous. But you've seen who wrote it? As if it wasn't obvious from part of the article, that is."

"Huh?"

Al ran his free hand through his hair, grimacing. "I'd have known even if her name hadn't been on the byline. Brooke Lingarten." He met James's eyes. "The date I had the other week who expected me to agree that homosexuality was akin to bestiality. Hence the quote about what I said. Not precisely my words, but..."

He looked away again. He'd known at the time he was being outrageously vulgar. Had done so deliberately. What he hadn't known was how vindictive Brooke could be...and what a particularly strong position she held, with her father owning the paper for which she wrote, to make best use of her vindictiveness. Al would have found it hard enough to deal with the things which had been written about him. He was not quite as thick-skinned as he liked to make out, and he was also concerned about the effect such accusations would have on his films, about which he cared deeply. Understandably—and Al sympathised massively with the feeling—many people would feel uncomfortable supporting independent films made by a sexual predator. He had to admit that were he reading the piece at face value, he would have exactly the same reaction. But his films dealt with important (to Al, hugely important) issues of mental health and gender identity. The thought that he himself would be the ruin of his own films was hard to take. Plus, as someone who—precisely *because* of his promiscuity—took consent issues with the utmost seriousness, the shock of practically being accused of assault was a deep one. It hit at the very heart of who Al was as a person. The fact that he had himself been raped only a year previously made the whole subject of sexual assault that little more personal, too. Al bit down on his lip, firmly banishing those memories. He still found them hard to cope with; probably always would.

Hardest of all right now, though, was what had been written about James and Laurie—Laurie, in particular. The worst thing was, Brooke had done her research very well, and phrased her article very carefully. There was precious little to object to apart from the implications. Laurie had undeniably known James and Al since they were ten years old. The fact that he hadn't started a relationship with James until James was twenty-two—and not slept with Al until some time after that—was beside the point, not to mention utterly unprovable. And, of course, Laurie did indeed teach eighteen-year-olds of varying degrees of naivety. He was, however, utterly uninterested in any of them in anything but an academic fashion. Al, quite frankly, was sometimes astounded that the apparently staid Laurie had found himself in a relationship with two men in the first place. The idea of him wanting anything more was as ridiculous as the same idea would have been about James—though thankfully the latter theory had not been suggested in black and white. James had only to live with the humiliation of this public 'outing'; but he would find that difficult enough, Al knew.

As to the allegations about Al, they were again impossible to disprove. The one specific claim had enough of an element of truth to be difficult to deny, especially as Al was essentially honest; the rest was all vague but malicious innuendo. Al could try proving that he was certainly not meeting such a wide range of people, but he suspected he would only serve to make himself look ridiculous without taking away from the general message of the piece. Insisting that all the sex he had was consensual and enjoyed by both (or all, on occasion) parties would be pointless: he would say that, after all, wouldn't he?

Al felt a sinking feeling in his gut. He dropped the paper on the table and walked away, facing the wall and kicking at it repeatedly. What the fuck were they going to do?

Chapter Four

LAURIE

The atmosphere in the flat was so heavy that it was almost painful as Laurie walked through the front door. It was one of those moments where you didn't need good instincts to know that something was horribly wrong: any fool could have told.

"What is it?" he demanded, looking around at his boyfriends.

James was standing looking down at a newspaper on a table. Laurie wasn't sure whether his lover was actually reading it, or just staring in its general direction. His face was pale. Al, meanwhile was kicking the wall over and over again, muttering "Shit, shit, shit" as he did so. He turned at Laurie's question.

"You'd better read that," he said, his voice closed and grim as he indicated the paper by James. He turned back to the wall, but instead of continuing to kick it, he just leaned his head against it, looking utterly defeated.

James moved over to allow Laurie to pick up the paper. "I'd ask how your day's been, but I don't think it's going to matter."

IIe sounded as bad as Al did. And when Laurie glanced at the paper, he immediately knew why. The headline was cruel and damning. *Altogether Sick: Film-Maker's Sordid Sex Romps*. This was not going to be an easy read for anyone who loved Al, as both Laurie and James did.

"Please don't kill me," Al said in a low voice, still facing the wall.

Laurie looked across at him, frowning. Al was the victim here, surely? Why was he looking quite so concerned about Laurie's response? Laurie realised for the first time that inset into the large picture of Al was a smaller one of himself. With increasing fear, he began to read. It did not take long until he came across the reference to himself, and looking through it, Laurie suddenly felt very ill.

The words on the page stared at him, certain phrases jumping out. "Known them intimately since they were ten years old"; "bedding two of them"; "suggests a fetish".

The implication was quite clear. 'Intimate' knowledge of ten-year-olds was not something any adult should be accused of. Putting the paper down suddenly, Laurie stumbled to the bathroom, locking the door behind him and sinking to crouching position. The sickness hit in a wave of nausea, and he leaned over the toilet, puking until his throat was raw with bile. Then he stayed there, his head resting on the rim of the seat, waiting for the shudders to stop running through him.

The article had made it sound—awful. Sick. Laurie hadn't quite realised how his relationship with James and Al might look from the outside. Not until he'd read it in the newspaper in black and white. *It suggests a fetish.* The words ran through his mind over and over again. *A fetish.* He knew the paper was sensationalising things, making them sound as bad as possible. It didn't help. They sounded bad. Laurie knew the word, was trying to avoid saying it, even inside his head. Paedophile. They'd made it sound as if he'd been—fuck knew—grooming ten-year-old kids to be some sort of sex slaves? About to do it to all of his students, as well, apparently. Dr Laurence Rose, the lecturer with a fetish for young boys. That was the sort of reputation that stuck, deserved or not. He felt more bile bubble up through his oesophagus, hot and painful, and swallowed hard.

"Laurie?" James's voice, uncertain, outside the bathroom door.

"Y—" Laurie's voice was gone, the acid having burned his throat. He turned on the cold water tap, cupped some in his hands, and drank, shuddering as the liquid went down. "Yes?"

"You okay?"

No. So very far from okay. "Yes," he said again.

How could he go out of the bathroom? How could he face James and Al after reading that? He was ashamed.

"Please, Laurie."

His gorgeous boyfriend—his gorgeous, young, boyfriend—*one* of his gorgeous young boyfriends (*fetish, it suggests a fetish*)—was pleading with him to come out, to stop hiding. Laurie bit his lip hard, tasted the blood in his mouth. It tasted better than the bile.

"Coming," he said, defeated.

He unlocked the door and stepped out, feeling himself shaking. James stood by the doorway, gazing at him with anxious eyes. Al was slumped on the sofa, arms wrapped round his legs in a childlike pose, looking vulnerably young and tiny. Laurie's stomach turned at the sight, and he repressed a shudder.

"Shit," Al said. "I'm so sorry."

Laurie stared at him, as if seeing him for the first time, and said nothing. How had he never realised quite how small, how fragile Al was? He flashed back on some of the things he'd done to and with Al, and looked away in a hurry, fearing he would be sick again. James put a hand on Laurie's arm, and Laurie fought the urge to shake it off. *Fetish.* He'd lusted after James since James was eighteen years old. It wasn't ten, but it wasn't good. It had been horribly inappropriate, as he'd known damn well at the time—especially as he'd first realised his attraction whilst living with another man, for god's sake. A man his own age, whom he'd split up with because he was obsessed with an eighteen-year-old *kid*. Laurie had managed to put all of that behind him, pretend that he was perfectly normal, that his relationship with James was fine. Completely fine, nothing wrong with it at all. He'd even normalised the fact that he was fucking James's best friend as well. It wasn't normal. He was a freak, and now it was public knowledge. That—and the sordid implications of more. Why wouldn't people believe the rest of it, when there was that much truth in it already?

Laurie turned back to the paper and read through the rest of it. That was all a slap at Al, accusing him—bloody hell—of sexual assault, pretty much. Certainly of taking advantage of vulnerable women. Anything less likely was hard to imagine. Laurie had seen the expression on Al's ex-partners' faces when they remembered their experiences with him: a pleased smile, a look of warmth and excited secrets. Most of them would probably be happy to be 'taken advantage of' again, were Al interested. Ridiculous lies, but hurtful and hard to counter. Al would find that difficult to cope with.

However, Laurie's eyes were drawn back to the paragraph about himself. It seemed sicker...and truer...every time he read it. He realised that James was speaking and he hadn't heard a word. He looked up.

"Sorry," he said. "I—um...well, I'll be back in a minute."

Without waiting for a reply, he walked into the bedroom and looked around, not really noticing what he was doing until he discovered he had a bag half-packed. Because he couldn't stay here. Not now. Not right now, not with those words hanging over him. He couldn't stay in this flat with two young men he'd known as children, sleep in the same bed as them. The thought was slightly sick. How had he managed to do it for so long without realising how wrong it was?

Razor. Toothbrush. He'd need to get them from the bathroom. Then he'd go. Quickly, before he could have second thoughts. The boys—the *boys*—had each other. They'd be fine. Laurie needed to get away, clear his head. Work out what the hell he was going to do about his job; what he could say to the university to persuade them that no, he truly wasn't seducing—or worse—his male students. Shit. The amount of times he'd had one-to-ones with eighteen-year-olds in his office, the door closed, and never thought twice about it. He couldn't prove he'd done nothing to them save talk about films (and sometimes, oh god, their private lives, if those had been impacting on their work). Laurie strode through to the bathroom, still half-dazed, and collected his bits, putting them in the bag.

"Laurie?" James's voice, strung up on tension. "What are you..." His boyfriend trailed off. It was clear enough what Laurie was doing.

"I need to get out. For a bit." Laurie didn't know how long. He didn't know anything right now.

"Please don't," James said softly.

Al was silent, unusually so. His face was white, and his eyes large and worried as he watched Laurie heft up his bag and walk towards the door. He looked somehow...diminished. *Young*, thought Laurie viciously. Because that's what he was. Young.

"Laurie!" James said again. He was right by Laurie now, his hands on Laurie's arms as if to prevent him from leaving by force.

"I-I can't..." Laurie looked blankly at James, as if seeing someone totally different. He found himself visualising the face of the ten-year-old he had once known, and then felt painfully ill. James's touch made him feel dirty.

"Laurie, don't do this to me. To us," James pleaded.

Al walked over and put his hand on James's arm in turn. He, too, looked pleadingly at Laurie, though he still didn't speak. Laurie bit his lips together hard. How could he stay here, with these two, when people were saying—had written— He swallowed hard, and swiped a kiss at James's mouth, at Al's forehead.

"I'm sorry," he whispered softly and he walked out.

FORTY-FIVE CONFUSED MINUTES later, Laurie found himself standing on Gillie's doorstep, his bag dumped in front of him. He rang the bell. Gillie answered within seconds.

"Laurie," she said, her face serious. She looked behind him. "No James or Al?"

Laurie shook his head. He swallowed. "Have you seen it?" he asked. Gillie nodded. Laurie held his hands out in front of him, in supplication. He noticed that they were shaking. "Gillie, I swear to god I never looked at James like that or anything until he was eighteen," he said, his voice wavering.

God, what was he doing here? With James's mother, for goodness sake. The trouble was, she was his best friend and she had been the only person he could think of to run to. The person he'd always run to when he was in trouble. And he was certainly in deep trouble now—more than ever. Because even the truth was awful enough—when James had been eighteen, Laurie had been twenty-eight. James had barely been an adult, where Laurie had been...shit, old enough to know better.

But Gillie's eyes were full of love and sympathy. "I know, darling. Come in." She reached out to take his trembling hands in her own and tugged him over the doorstep. "Oh, Laurie," she sighed, pulling him close. "It's okay. It's okay."

He sank his head down onto her shoulder, his eyes filling with tears of relief. "God, Gillie, what am I going to do?" He cast a quick look back out the door. "Can I stay?" he asked, hesitantly. "I—I couldn't..."

"Come in," Gillie said again. There was the hint of a sigh in her tone for a second, but then it was gone so that Laurie wasn't sure whether it was just his paranoia. "I'm not going to turn you away, am I?" She paused, letting go of Laurie so that he could rescue his bag. "Does James know where you are? Or that you've gone, at any rate?"

Laurie nodded. "He's safe with Al. I spoke to them...kissed them goodbye." His voice cracked a little, despite himself.

"Okay." She took his bag from him and put it by the stairs. "Sorry, lovely. I had to ask."

"I know. I shouldn't have come."

"Of course you should. You're my best friend." Gillie led him into the sitting room. "Now, wine or whiskey? I think we're past the realms of a cup of tea."

"Yes," agreed Laurie, wholeheartedly.

She cocked a shrewd look at him. "Whiskey." When they were settled with their drinks, she spoke again. "Laurie, love, it's only scurrilous gossip. It's aimed at Al more than you. Can't you just ignore it?"

"How can I? How could anyone?" Laurie sipped his drink, frightened to take too much in case he couldn't stop, in case he went on drinking until he passed out. Then again, maybe that was the best option. Except it would hardly be fair on Gillie. "Gillie, they said I was..." He couldn't finish the sentence.

"They didn't. And anyone who knows you knows it's not true. Laurie, do you think I'd be letting you through my front door if there was any truth in any of that nonsense? I love you dearly, but this is my son—my *sons*," Gillie corrected herself, "we are talking about."

Despite the fact there was no official relationship between Gillie and Al, Laurie knew that as far as Gillie was concerned, Al was family. He always had been, even before she knew he was dating her actual son. Laurie's best friend was a wonderful woman. Very like her biological son in some ways; but even that tiny reference of James made him feel uncomfortable right now. Why had he had to fall for someone he'd known as a kid? Why, oh why, had he then fallen for *two* people he'd known as kids? (*Fetish. Fetish. Fetish.*)

"I don't know. Maybe...maybe it's right," Laurie said shakily.

"Don't be ridiculous," Gillie snapped. "It's nonsense. Stop it!"

"They are much younger than me, and—"

"And there's a twenty-year age gap between my Head of Department and his wife and no one bats an eyelid," Gillie finished. "You're all of age."

Laurie groaned. "'All'. That's another thing."

"Well, that is unconventional," Gillie admitted. "I know I asked what the neighbours would say when you first told me, but I didn't really anticipate an answer like this. But that's really no one's business but your own, after all."

"The thing is, Gillie..." Laurie felt himself flushing red with embarrassment and humiliation. "There's other stuff you don't know, too. Maybe..."

"Maybe what?"

"Maybe the—the *fetish* stuff is true."

"It isn't," Gillie said firmly. "You love James and Al, don't you?"

"Of course I do. But the thing..." Laurie stood up, facing away from her. "The thing is, sometimes... God, I can't believe I'm even saying this... Sometimes I make Al—oh fuck." He buried his head in his hands. "Make him do...things," he finished, his voice muffled, humiliation and shame warring inside him.

"Against his will?" Gillie's voice was sharp.

Laurie took his head out of his hands and spun to face her, horrified. "What the... Jesus Christ, Gillie, of *course,* not against his w—"

He caught sight of her face. She was smiling at him. Not a smile of amusement, but one of sympathy and understanding. "Exactly," she said softly. "Laurie, dearest, that makes all the difference." She stood up and went to him, stroking his arm. "Lovely, I don't ask about your sex life because it's my son—and my adopted son, now, too—you're sleeping with and—well, that. There are some things a mother doesn't need to know—and still more that her son needs to know that his mother doesn't know! But you know, from when we were younger and Terry was still alive. Our sex, mine and his, wasn't always precisely vanilla." She smiled reminiscently now. "Anything but. There's nothing wrong with having interesting sex with consensual partners, you know."

"Even if they're so much younger than I am?"

They made their way back to the sofa. Gillie kissed his cheek. "You're ten years older than them, not forty years older. And they're twenty-five. Quite old enough to make their own minds up, wouldn't you think? Besides"—she smiled—"I can't imagine anyone doing anything to Al against his will." Laurie winced suddenly, thinking of a winter's day approximately a year previously, and Gillie looked at him hard. "What?"

Laurie took a deep breath. "You might as well know. Al was...well, raped about a year back. That's when he started living with us. And why. Sort of. James and I freaked out about him living alone, no one knowing whether he was safe," he admitted.

"*What?*" Gillie was horrified. "One of his dates?"

Laurie bit his lip, shaking his head. It had been worse than that. "Um, no. A—a group of men cornered him, beat him up fairly badly." He remembered the way Al had looked on their doorstep that night, shaking and bruised. The fierce surge of protectiveness and anger which had run through Laurie. It had been the first inkling that Laurie had got that his feelings for Al were more than those of simple friendship and sexual attraction. "Just"—he gave a mirthless laugh —"'just' his mouth, the rape. But..." He trailed off.

"Why was I never told about this?" Gillie demanded, sounding torn between distress and anger. "I'm the nearest thing he has to a mother, for goodness sake."

Laurie squeezed her hand. "I know. He— Don't speak to him about it, Gillie. He can't talk about it. I don't think anyone knows except James and me, and the police."

"You went to the police, then?"

"Yeah." Laurie paused. "He was very brave, Gill. It was...pretty horrific. Oh, I think Gemma might know as well, actually."

Gillie frowned. "Gemma?"

"Al's..." Laurie broke off. "Ah," he said thoughtfully. They had never claimed that they were exclusive in their relationship, James and Laurie and Al—but he knew that most people would have presumed that they were, if they knew they were together. James and Laurie certainly slept with no one save each other and Al. Al, however, was a very different kettle of fish. Laurie wasn't quite sure how Gillie would take the rest of this sentence. The newspaper had gone on about Al's varied sex life, but whether Gillie had believed it was true was another matter, especially given the clear lies about his 'violation' of women. She knew what Al *had* been like, certainly—hence her question about his date—but did she know that some things had not changed? "Sort of Al's girlfriend," he finished, looking nervously at Gillie.

"I beg your pardon?" Gillie's eyebrows had risen. She didn't sound angry, precisely, but certainly disconcerted.

"*One* of Al's girlfriends," Laurie corrected himself, ruefully. "Though mostly they're not...not what you'd call girlfriends, precisely. Like you said, 'dates'. But Gemma's a friend, too—James and I have met her a few times." He sat through thirty seconds of interminable silence with Gillie. "Um, we're okay about it, you know," he offered tentatively. "James and I. It was agreed from the start. He isn't cheating on us."

"But you and James..." Gillie broke off, perhaps realising the infelicitous nature of this questioning.

"For what it's worth, James and I are exclusive, yes," Laurie said, answering her anyway. She had at least earned that right for taking Laurie in. "Were," he added, a frown settling between his eyes. "God, I don't know what to do."

"Not sleep around," snapped Gillie at this.

Laurie winced away at the anger in her voice. "Gillie, I—"

Gillie had sucked her lips between her teeth. "Laurie," she said carefully, "I knew when you and James got together that there was a reasonable chance that it might one day go wrong. Relationships don't always last forever. I know that. And you're my best friend." She took a breath. "But James is my son. I can cope with a relationship break-up, and love you both. But so help me, Laurie, if you do anything to hurt James that you don't need to have done, I'm not ever going to be able to forgive that. This thing with Al, I've been happy for you because I could see it was what you all wanted. But if you sleep with anyone else, James will be devastated. Do you understand me?"

Laurie had known Gillie fifteen years and never heard her sound like this before. He felt himself wanting to cower from her as she spoke. But at the same time, she was so far from the truth that it was almost farcical.

"God, that's the last thing I'm going to do," he said. He wasn't sure whether it was a laugh or a sob which he gave before he spoke next. "It's whether I should be in James's life at all which is worrying me. As you said, why would someone like him want someone like me?"

Gillie softened immediately. "No, Laurie, that's not what I said," she corrected gently. "My son adores you, and I know perfectly well why. But you have his heart. Be careful with it. Please? And," she added, "for what it's worth, look after Al, too. He's much more fragile than he'd try to have you believe. Though it sounds like you already know that." She gave a small smile. "I worry about my second son almost as much as my first, you know," she admitted. "And my best friend?" She held her hands out to Laurie, and he put his hands in hers without a moment's hesitation. "I worry about him, too."

Chapter Five

AL

Seen the article. You OK?

Al looked down at the text from his girlfriend, Gemma. Across at James, who was staring at the front door as if he could force Laurie to come back through it if only he looked long enough. Was he okay? Well, *there* was a question and a half.

Gemma. She was hardly going to want to see him, at least for the moment. Even if she didn't believe the worst of the allegations—and Al was pretty sure she knew he wasn't a sexual predator, at any rate—it would hardly do her, or any of them, in fact, any good to get herself mixed up with any of it. Al had checked the Internet, briefly, googling his name; the top results all seemed to relate to the article. Add a singer from a famous band, and the hits would go up to sky-high levels. Thank fuck that Brooke hadn't caught up with that little snippet of information.

Yeah, he texted. *Understand you won't want to be in contact for a while. No hard feelings. Best of love.*

It was surprising how hard the text was to write. Gemma and Al were much more than just bed partners. They had a strong and genuine friendship, but there were certain things no one could be expected to accept. Al felt his chest constrict; then looked again at James, reminding himself what he'd managed to do to him. To his best friend and love. One of Al's loves had left them—left his own fucking flat, for god's sake. The other was sitting looking as if his entire world had just caved in. And it was Al's fault, and no one else's. God, he was a fuck-up. He turned the phone off; if Laurie were to contact one of them—if—it would be James, not him. And there was no point waiting for further bad news. Al took a moment to try to remember who else had his mobile number, and decided there was no point. It was switched off now. They could all wait to berate him.

"Jamie," he said softly, going over to him and touching his shoulder gently.

James nodded, not looking up. Al took this as permission to sit down next to him.

"Say something," Al said. "Tell me I'm a bastard. That you hate me. That you want me to leave. Yell at me."

"Not—your—fault," said James thickly, as he had done before.

It was, though, and that was the hell of it. If Al didn't sleep around, this wouldn't have happened. Heck, if Al had been able to resist using his sharp tongue to slap down someone who said something hurtful to him, this wouldn't have happened. A bit of self-control, and everyone would be fine. Instead of which, Al had opened his big mouth and...

"I'm sorry."

"He left."

Al could hear the heartbreak in James's voice, and there was nothing he could do about it. "He'll come back."

"You think?"

"He just needs to talk to someone. He'll have gone to Gillie. Your mum'll make him see sense. He loves you, Jamie."

James made a noise which was half-laugh, half-sob. "You reckon? At the moment, I'm finding it a bit hard to get past the fact that he just walked out and left me. Makes it hard to feel that loved."

"I know," Al whispered, pulling James into his arms. "I know. But it's true. Hey," he added, trying to joke, "Laurie hasn't been putting up with my crap for as long as you have. Not everyone finds it that easy to cope with, you know."

James lay his head on Al's shoulder. "Not. Your. Fault," he said for the third time. "Fuck's sake, Al, it's a load of bollocks, full of lies. You know that as well as I do. As well as Laurie does."

Al wasn't sure whether it was better or worse that James was being so forgiving. It was a relief to know that he wasn't completely beyond the pale to both of his boyfriends. If, indeed, Laurie was still prepared to be his boyfriend after this. It seemed unlikely that he would want that. Cold dread seeped into his chest. Al couldn't believe that Laurie would leave James—it wasn't possible—but Al? And where did that leave the three of them? Plus, part of Al would feel a little better if James would only scream at him. This silent despair was awful.

He wished they knew where Laurie had actually gone—he must be at Gillie's, surely? But would he really turn to James's mother after walking out on her son? However, Laurie hadn't even sent James a text, as far as Al knew. Given all of that, though; knowing both that it was his fault and yet despite that James, even now, even with Laurie fuck knew where, was refusing to blame him... Well, perhaps that was Al's punishment in itself, knowing that he didn't deserve the loyalty James was offering so unreservedly. It certainly hurt enough.

The two of them slept in Al's bed that night. Or, rather, in the one which used to be Al's, before they'd agreed that all three of them sharing together was a better plan, given the huge size of Laurie's and James's bed.

Given that they were, apparently, in love.

James had only previously slept in Al's bed on a couple of rare occasions—the first night Al moved in, when they'd all three shared his new one (a bad plan: it was a standard-sized double, and not only were there three of them in it, but both James and Laurie were tall men), and one time later when James had woken Al from a nightmare and spent the rest of the night curled around him as if he could physically prevent further bad dreams by his close presence. Al's nightmares had become considerably less common since he'd been sharing with Laurie and James, so who knew? Perhaps James had been on to something. Certainly Al had not dreamt of anything bad for the rest of that particular night. But James had taken one stricken look at the door of the room they usually slept in and turned to Al.

"The other room? Please?"

Al nodded, comprehending that James couldn't bear to sleep in the bed he'd always shared with Laurie. The flat had, after all, been Laurie's originally: first James, and then Al, had been invited to move in. Al, he remembered with a painful tug of the heart, had practically been ordered so to do, at least temporarily. But 'their' bedroom was first and foremost Laurie's bedroom. It was understandable that James couldn't bear to sleep there without his boyfriend—without the man he'd been hopelessly in love with since he was sixteen years of age. From time to time over the last few hours, Al had wondered how he would manage to live with the guilt if Laurie didn't come back. Al was James's best friend, and they loved each other dearly on a level far beyond that of friends. But Laurie? Laurie had something of James's that no one else could ever reach; something so precious that if he ever rejected it, James would never give it to another man in the rest of his life. Did Laurie have any fucking idea how important he was to James? Al was inclined to think not, despite the fact that the older man usually looked at James with an expression close to worship in his own eyes.

And that was it, really, wasn't it? The obvious statement of what—or rather, who—the problem was. Al. Al was the problem. James's love for Laurie was beyond compare; beyond anything Al could ever consider. If he wrote a film about it, Al thought wryly, he would be criticised for over-sentimentality—a critique rarely aimed in his direction. He was hardly known as the last of the great romantics. And Laurie had always been so very fond—adoring—of James. Al had been...not jealous, when he first realised that he was in love with them both, but regretful. Melancholy. It had seemed too good to be true when they had assured him that they loved him back.

And it *had* been too good to be true, it seemed. James and Laurie had been together for what—coming up to four years? Over three and a half, certainly. Granted, they'd been having sex with Al occasionally for more than two of those years—bloody hell, that was a bit of a shock to realise in itself!—but they'd been a couple with an occasional extra sex partner up until the last six months or so. A stable, happy couple. Then they'd taken him into their love, and now this. James, lying on the bed pretending to be asleep when Al knew damn well he wasn't. Laurie, god knew where—presumably Gillie's house.

But without Al...without Al, James and Laurie could have a normal relationship. A happy one. Two people in love, just as it was always written that it should be. Granted they were both blokes, but in this day and age that was hardly outrageous. Al blinked up at the ceiling regretfully, and knew what the answer was. He turned over in bed.

He turned over, and James turned towards him, whispering, "Please, Al. Please. I need you."

"I'm here." Al leaned in and kissed him. "I'm here."

"Yes."

James was kissing him back, hard and desperate, clinging to him suddenly as if adrift on a raft of emotions which were threatening to overwhelm him. Al gave as good as he got, stroking James's back with bitten-nail fingertips, undulating his body against his lover's.

"It's okay," Al soothed.

"Al, please..."

"I will."

"Fuck me," James begged. "Please. I need you to."

Al felt himself tense up. He bit down on his lip, hard, because James had asked the one thing that Al couldn't—wouldn't—do. He held James closer still, pressing him as tightly against himself as physically possible.

"I can't, Jamie," he said regretfully.

Not because he didn't want to. God, he'd wanted to fuck James for years. But it wasn't right. No one fucked James except Laurie. They never had, ever. That was how James had always wanted it. How he still wanted it, in his heart. But Laurie wasn't here.

"Please. I need—"

"I know what you need," Al said, sadly. "Or who. But I'm not him, James."

"I know. Just this once..." James pleaded.

"Oh, Jamie." Al felt like his heart was breaking. "Anything. Anything but this. Something you won't regret in the morning, lover."

Because Al knew that above all. He could fuck James now, easily. James was begging him to. And tomorrow, when James woke up, he'd hate himself. He'd hate Al, too, but Al could cope with that more easily. What he couldn't cope with was the pain of self-hatred which James would go through. The regrets. The guilt. The knowledge he'd done something he could never take back. Al kissed James hard on the mouth, wanting to be able to push the hurt that his boyfriend was feeling away, knowing he couldn't.

"Anything else," he whispered hopelessly to James.

"Oh god," said James, and he *sounded* like his heart was breaking; probably because it was.

Al couldn't fuck him, but he could try to bring him some level of forgetfulness. Some distraction from the aching heart and mind. He was usually more inclined to let Laurie or James take the lead in bed, but he knew that wasn't what James needed right now. He needed someone to do it for him, to pull him into a state of arousal where everything but his body was forgotten. Al remembered Laurie saying, once: *James likes to feel a bit of weight on top of him*, so he rolled onto his boyfriend, pinning him down underneath his body and rocking against him, kissing him over and over. They frotted against each other until they were both hard, and Al was moaning against James as he kissed him.

"Turn over," he whispered to James. "Lie on your front." James gave him a long look, and Al smiled at him lovingly. "Trust me."

James rolled over, and Al grabbed the lube, smoothing it over his cock until he was wet and slippery. Then he lay on top of James's back, rubbing his cock into the cleft in James's arse. He wouldn't fuck him, but he could do this much. It couldn't hurt, could it? He had a sudden visualisation of how it would feel to fuck James and gave a little groan. His cock rubbed over James's entrance, teasing them both. So close, so close. James, god. He sucked and nibbled James's back as he thrust against him, and James was murmuring something encouraging under his breath, which brought an unexpectedly choky feeling to Al's throat. God, he loved James so damn much. He slid his arms around his lover, one under his chest and the other further down, his hand, lube-sticky, grasping James's cock in warm fingers.

"Fuck yourself on me and the bed," he encouraged. "Come on, Jamie. Let me bring us both off like this."

"Al."

James said his name, nothing more, but began to move, humping up against the mattress as Al pushed fast and hard against his arse, his cock pressing in the indentation, pointing down towards James's balls so that the head almost touched them with every stroke, sliding through the warm crease between James's buttocks.

"God, yes, like that. Jamie, god. Love you so much. Fuck. Come on, Jamie, give it up for me. Yes, Jamie, god, yes."

James was groaning and rutting harder, and Al could hear more and more words falling out of his own mouth, almost without his own volition, as they both came closer and closer to the edge. Al came first, spilling himself down James's arse, and panting hard against his back. James followed, as if the feeling of Al's orgasm was what he needed for his own. He jerked and moaned, and there was an electric moment when they were both still high as kites on the feeling. Then Al rolled off, pulling James into his arms and holding him gentle and close. There were warm tears against his shoulder, but James didn't acknowledge them and Al said nothing. He just held James until he felt his boyfriend's body relax into sleep, and then held him some more as Al lay awake, following painful thoughts down the track he knew now he needed to follow. Finally, Al, too, slept.

AL WOKE IN the morning to a text from Gemma. It said, simply:

Don't be an idiot, and had been sent shortly after his response the previous evening. Apparently, she had been made more sympathetic by his continued lack of reply, as there was a further one written a couple of hours later. *OK, I admit I don't want to get into the papers. Text me, and we'll meet somewhere private. You OK?*

Al blinked. James had barely slept, he knew—and James was usually a champion sleeper. He'd dozed off to start with, but every time Al woke in the night (which had been often), he'd been aware of James beside him, staring up at the ceiling of the darkened room. His love had finally fallen into a deeper sleep around six a.m., so Al had left him to lie as long as he possibly could, sliding carefully out of bed without waking him.

He looked at the texts from Gemma again and felt grateful for her warmth and honesty. He could feel her friendship, even in the earlier one berating him as an idiot—could almost hear her voice saying it. Al, despite his lifestyle, was essentially a private person, but Gemma was closer to him than most people, so with a need to unburden himself, he replied:

Thanks. Laurie left last night. My fault.

Whilst he waited for a reply, he checked the rest of his texts. Nothing from Laurie, but then he'd hardly expected there would be. Whether Laurie was ever going to speak to him again, let alone forgive him, was up in the air. Al could hardly blame him if he didn't. One from Kaz, another semi-regular lover of Al's, bluntly asking him to delete his phone number. That hurt. One from Gillie, sending love. She said nothing about Laurie. Five from friends, telling him in one form of words or another that they knew it was all nonsense. At least Al wasn't going to be left high and dry by everyone, then. That was something. He'd half expected a text from Fen, his boss at the wine shop, but there was nothing. No voicemail, either. He'd have to go in and see her, discover if he still had a job. Could being accused of sexual deviancy get you sacked? Bringing the business into disrepute? Al thought not, legally, but if Fen wanted him to go, he would. She'd been good to him—he didn't want to damage her shop. She could hardly help it if he was a liability. And she could hardly be expected to watch her business go down the drain, just to keep employing a washed up film-maker who allegedly violated women.

The phone rang. Gemma's number.

"What the hell?" she demanded when he answered.

"You saw what they wrote," he said, not bothering to pretend he didn't know what she meant.

"Yes, but...what do you mean, left?" Gemma had always had a bit of a crush on Laurie, Al suspected. "He can't just have walked out."

"He did it nicely," Al said weakly. "Kissed us goodbye."

Al was clinging to the memory of that kiss, though he was aware that whilst James's had been to the lips, Laurie had merely brushed one across Al's forehead. Would Laurie get more or less angry with Al over time? Had he realised by now, properly, how much it was Al's fault—how much everything was always Al's fault? God, no wonder Al's parents had disliked him. James had always defended him, and look where that had got his best friend.

As if reading Al's mind, Gemma said, "James?"

"Don't."

There was a silence. "Al, honey, I need to see you."

"You can tell me to fuck off over the phone," Al said, trying not to sound bitter.

"I told you before not to be an idiot," Gemma said warningly. "Don't be an idiot."

"I can't leave Jamie." Al thought about how this sounded. "I don't mean he's suicidal or anything. I just mean, he's asleep right at the moment. And I need to know he's okay when he wakes. I can't do anything until—"

"No. That's fine," Gemma said quickly. "I don't want you to."

"Laurie will come back," Al said. "He won't leave James like this."

"Or you."

Al winced, glad she couldn't see him. "He won't leave James like this," he said again. "Look, Gem, just make sure no one knows you know me, okay?"

"As if I—"

"I care," he interrupted.

She sighed. "Yeah. So do I. I wish I didn't, but I do. Al, darling, I'm here. Don't you dare cut me off. I mean it. Look after yourself. And I'm here. You'd better text me every day, or I'll start stalking you, and then you'll regret it."

"Gem," Al said, a glimpse of his normal self peeking through, "if I thought I could get you to stalk me, I'd be tempted." He turned serious. "Thanks, though. I've lost one lover so far; well, two. I hope Laurie's coming back, but I've definitely lost another. I'll keep in touch, as long as you're still prepared to talk to me."

"Idiot," she said for the third time. "Take care, love. I'll be waiting to hear."

"Yeah. You're a good friend."

"You're not so bad yourself," she retorted, before she cut the connection.

James woke shortly after that, quiet but coping, though ruefully admitting that he felt like hell. He didn't mention Laurie, and Al didn't quite dare. Al nonetheless persuaded him not to go in to work that day; James looked as if the least thing might be the final straw, and if truth be told, Al wanted him somewhere where he could look after him. Al himself had been intending to work on the script for his next film. With the paper saying what it had, however, he hadn't the heart. Who would go to see it anyway, even if the production company could be persuaded to take it? In the early afternoon, he left James playing his guitar and went to see Fen. He'd considered phoning, but this was a conversation best done in person, Al reckoned, and James seemed safe to leave.

'James seemed safe to leave.' It was hardly the most positive statement one could make about one's lover: that you could leave him in the house alone for a short while without the fear of coming back to a corpse. Al hated himself rather a lot as he walked down to see Fen.

Fen looked up in surprise when Al walked into the shop.

"What are you doing here? You're not shifted on to work until tomorrow."

Al glanced at Daisy, who was working behind the till. "Hi Daisy," he said. Then, as she nodded and grinned a response, he turned to Fen. "Can I speak to you next door?" he asked, indicating the office.

"Sure. You're not having a raise, so Daisy, don't get any ideas," Fen said firmly. They went next door and Fen shut the door. "Resigning?" she asked.

"Do you want me to?" Al replied, his heart sinking. He'd worried...but then when he'd arrived, he'd thought, from the way Fen had greeted him, that maybe things weren't so bad after all. Perhaps she just hadn't wanted to chew him out in front of Daisy. That would be like her—she was a firm boss, but kind, in her way.

"What did you say?" Fen asked.

"I will, if you ask me to."

Al had had plenty of time to think things over. Plenty of things to think over, mind, too. But it had been a long night. A very, very, long night.

"Why should I want that?" Fen asked, clearly genuinely confused. "It was the only reason I could think of for this cloak and dagger privacy business. I hoped the filming was doing so well you could throw me over for it. I take it that's not the case?"

Al gave a hollow laugh. "Hardly." He leaned on her desk. "Fen, haven't you seen the paper?"

That was an eventuality he hadn't anticipated. Somehow he'd felt like everyone must have seen it—everyone who knew him, anyway. The idea that he'd have to take someone else through it all over again was pretty awful.

"What, that article?" Fen sat down in her chair, leaned back until it creaked, and stared at Al. "Load of old shite," she said dismissively. "You surely didn't think I'd be bothered?"

Her disbelief did weird things to Al. He felt as if his skin was all prickly, his legs somewhat tremulous. To him and his, the article had been a devastating disaster. Those around him had reacted in various ways, but everyone had been affected. That his boss was taking it so very much in her stride was a shock. Al could see that the article might not be the end of the world to everybody, but to see it as totally irrelevant was beyond him just at the moment. Nonetheless, it was reassuring— and strangely touching—to have it treated in this way.

"Well, I..."

"That's why you're here today?"

Fen was in her late fifties, a brisk, efficient woman who had been running her own business for seventeen years. She'd taken Al on when he'd still been a student, looking for a summer job, then employed him permanently when he came back a year later, university finished. That had been nearly four years ago, and he'd been working for her ever since. She treated Al with the same cool practicality that she showed everyone, but for once there was an unusually soft expression on her face.

He nodded.

"Al," she said slowly, "you've done nothing wrong. I already knew you slept around—excuse me for putting it so bluntly. But we've had enough of your ex-lovers through the shop, after all." She raised an eyebrow at him. "I should perhaps thank you for drumming up business; there have been enough of them that I'm pretty sure you must be saying something good about us. If you were the sort of dubious character the paper suggested, I suspect you mightn't be on such good terms with so many of them. Besides all that, you're good at your job, you're reliable, and I enjoy having you around the place. And no," she added, a note of her usual severity back in her voice, "you're still not getting a raise. Now, get out of my sight and stop interrupting my work. Come back tomorrow when you're due."

"Fen," Al said, a lump in his throat, "thanks."

She flapped a hand at him. "Out. Out."

Al managed perhaps his first genuine smile since he'd originally read the article, and left.

Chapter Six

LAURIE

Laurie stayed at Gillie's house for the next two days, calling in sick to work and hiding from the world. He knew it was cowardly, and that at some point he would have to make a decision about what to do next. But for the life of him, he couldn't bring himself to do it quite yet. Gillie had agreed with him about work: she took one look at him the morning after his arrival and said gently, "I don't think you're in a fit state, Laurie dear," and let him be. When she arrived home that evening to discover Laurie still there, she said nothing and just cooked for him. Like her son, Laurie thought again, with a pang, she was a very good cook.

But at lunchtime on the second day—Friday—Laurie checked his personal email account. There was a message from Al, titled briefly *Please Read*. Laurie looked at it for a long time, before berating himself for being such a coward and opening it. The text was simple.

Laurie,

Please come back. James needs you.

I know you must blame me.

I'll leave. I think—no, I know—Gillie will have me for a while. We can swap houses. I gather from James that's where you are.

Please, Laurie, I'm begging you. Come back to James.

Al

Laurie read the message through five times over. He hated himself, if possible, even more after reading it. Looking at what he'd done not only to James, the subject of the message, but to Al, the writer. *Blame... I'll leave... I'm begging you...* Had Laurie blamed Al? Certainly the article had been written because of Al's position as a film-maker, so perhaps he could be held responsible to that degree. But blame—save for self-blame—had not really crossed Laurie's mind. He had been too appalled at seeing what was written about him in public view; too appalled at what his life looked like to an outsider to think of being angry at Al. Al was Al—frustrating, mercurial, amazing, and very, very much himself. Laurie had known him (he winced at the reminder) for fifteen years, after all. He had few misapprehensions about the younger man after all this time. His heart twinged. Those that he did have had tended to be to Al's detriment rather than in his favour.

And James? Oh god, James. James, whom Al said "needed" him; and if anyone would know that sort of thing, it would be Al. Except that on this particular occasion, Al was wrong. James needed Laurie like he needed a hole in the head. At the same time...the idea of life without James was horrific. And Laurie had an awful feeling that he was beginning to feel the same way about Al, too.

Which begged the question of what he was doing here, hiding from the people he loved the most. If the worst thing he could think of in life was losing them, why was he running away from James and Al? And whether long-term he should stay with them or not, the least he could do was to go back now and support them through what was not exactly the easiest time in either of his boyfriends' lives. Gillie had not criticised, nor even demanded when Laurie was going to be leaving, but she must be wondering, too. It wasn't as if his partners were strangers to her, after all. Her son and another young man she considered 'as good as'. Her forbearance with him had been admirable—and astounding—but she deserved better, too. She deserved to know that he was doing his best for his best friend's children.

And maybe Laurie deserved something, too. Maybe he deserved to know that whatever the outcome, he had done his best for those he loved. Whether their relationship survived or not, he could at least hold his head up high and know that he had not merely left them to suffer alone—that he had gone back, and tried to repair the damage he might have done. And apologised...no, grovelled, damn it...for leaving. He owed them all that much.

Unable to wait for Gillie to come back from work, at six o'clock Laurie left, leaving behind a long explanatory note and a bunch of flowers. He was scared that if he put his return off, he would lose his courage and back out, and he honestly wasn't sure he could live with himself if he did that. As it was, he felt ridiculously nervous as he turned the key in his own door. He wasn't sure if anyone would be at home. He wasn't sure what he'd say if they were.

Pushing the door open, he heard James say in a low voice, "Hey, Al."

James was on the far side of the room, his back to Laurie. He had one of his guitars in his lap, but he wasn't playing it, just holding it, his head resting on his hand. Laurie couldn't see his face, but his posture was one of utter despair, and Laurie felt something in his chest dissolve at the sight. He walked up to James, sliding both of his arms around his lover, and resting his head on James's.

"Hey," he said in turn.

James jerked, turning suddenly. The guitar slipped from his grasp and Laurie reached out and grabbed it hastily, lowering it carefully to the ground. James loved that particular guitar and would be devastated if anything happened to it. But James barely seemed to notice. He was just staring at Laurie with a pleading hope on his face.

"Laurie?"

Laurie shut his eyes for a second and held James close. "I'm sorry," he said. "I'm so sorry I left."

Before James could reply or Laurie find anything to add to the words, the door went again. This time it *was* Al. Both men looked over at him, and Laurie watched the emotions cross another man's face at the sight of him. For a second, Al's expression lit up with joy; then, as quickly as it had come, it was gone again. Al dumped down the carrier bag he was holding and gave Laurie a weak smile.

"Hi Laurie. I'll be five minutes, and then I'll be out of here, okay?"

"What?" demanded James sharply.

Al's voice was deliberately matter of fact. "Don't worry, Jamie. Just something Laurie and I agreed on. He'll be here and I'm going to take up residence with your mum for a bit. She'll have me, won't she? Always an open door for the prodigal. It's not a problem, I'd just intended to be gone before Laurie got here but I didn't know..."

"Laurie," James said dangerously, "what have you done?"

Laurie held James tight for a few seconds more and then let go, moving across the room to Al. "Al," he said softly. He took Al's hand and then went down on his knees by the young man's side. "Don't. Please. I'm sorry."

Al's hand trembled a little in his. "I don't understand."

"Nor do I," James put in.

It felt odd on his knees. Laurie was usually only in this pose when he was sucking one of his boyfriends off. He made Al kneel for him so often; it was curious to have the positions reversed. He felt strangely vulnerable.

"*You* said you'd go," he said to Al. "I didn't say I wanted you to." He hesitated. "I know I've been a coward, and I'm sorry. I ran away, like an utter bastard, when I should have been supporting you." He looked round at James. "Both of you. Forgive me."

"Don't you hate me?" Al asked, sounding curiously uncertain.

Laurie bent his head forward, resting it against their clasped hands. "You haven't done anything wrong."

"Come and sit down," James said, unexpectedly practical.

He stood up and walked over to them. Then he rested his hand on Laurie's shoulder for a second, as if making sure he was really there. Al was still shaking, just the tiniest bit. Laurie could feel it. They sat on the sofa together, all three of them.

"I shouldn't have left," Laurie said. "Not when you were in trouble. I'm so sorry. Please forgive me for that."

He was choosing his words with care. Truthfully, he was still unsure what the future held. But for the near future at least, his younger lovers deserved all the support he could give them. All the support he had failed, coward-like, to give them so far.

"No," said James softly. "You shouldn't."

"Just throwing me out would have been easier," Al added.

"No, it wouldn't have been," James retorted to this, giving Al a glare.

"No, it wouldn't have been," Laurie agreed.

He watched as Al flicked a quick glance at James and then looked down. "Well," Al said, trying for cheerfulness, "you're here now."

"Yes. And if I can make it up to you both, I will."

"How's work been?" Al looked like he both did and didn't want to ask.

"I've not been into the uni yet since the article came out," Laurie admitted, feeling like even more of a weakling than he had before. "Honestly, I still don't know what to do. I've basically been publicly accused of trying to seduce my students, as well as having sex with underage boys. Potentially, *extremely* underage boys." He felt the familiar shiver of nausea sweep through him.

"But it's not true," James objected.

"Yeah, but in my line of work, it's not a good accusation to have hanging around." Laurie grimaced. "I've deleted my Twitter account. I don't know if either of you...?" He left the question hanging.

Al sighed. "Yes, I've had some...interesting trolls," he admitted. "You can't sue the paper, either, because they carefully don't actually come out and say any of that. You *have* known us since we were ten, and you *do* teach eighteen-year-old students." He ran a hand over his face. "No point denying about you and Jamie being in a relationship, as everyone knows you're a couple. But you can deny the rest. It was going to be a lot easier if I wasn't living here, but even so—plenty of people have lodgers. It doesn't mean they're sleeping with them. Just deny it all." He gave a brief mirthless laugh. "As the rest of the article spends its time basically accusing me of sexually assaulting women, or at the very least, being pretty close to an unpaid prostitute, no one will be surprised that you're not in a relationship with me."

"No," said Laurie.

"Harsh but fair, I suppose," Al commented, wincing slightly at the firmness of Laurie's statement.

Laurie gritted his teeth. "I don't mean 'No, no one will be surprised', you idiot. I mean 'No, I'm not denying it.'" He glared at Al. "I am dating you. I know I've acted like an utter coward so far, so it's fair enough you don't expect anything more of me. But I won't do it."

"Well done." James whispered the words to Laurie, quietly enough that Al wouldn't hear. He kissed his ear.

Laurie flushed; even James had believed he'd lie about Al to protect himself. It didn't make Laurie feel all that great about himself. Especially as he didn't know how long he'd be dating either of them. But he was damned if he'd lie about it in advance. Right now, they were both his boyfriends. The fact they might not be in the near future was his own private agony. The papers could fuck right off about knowing about that.

"It'll be a lot easier for you," Al said.

Laurie looked at him shrewdly. "And for you?" he asked. Al looked away. "Quite," Laurie said. "So I'm to dump you in it for my own selfish sake, yes? It's okay for me to take my pleasure with you, but as soon as it gets difficult I'll just get shot of you."

"Ouch," James commented.

"It doesn't sound very nice when you put it like that," Al admitted. "But I do sleep around. Most people would consider that grounds for not calling what we have a relationship."

"Fuck it, I'm not most people," Laurie retorted. "I'm in love with you and I'm in love with James, and I need to man up and have the balls to deal with any fallout from that." He wondered, guiltily, whether he should have said that out loud, in the circumstances. If he wasn't going to stay with them; if he or they decided they were better off without him...was he making things more confusing with a declaration like that? But maybe, after how he'd behaved, both of them needed to hear it. They had to cope with the here and now before worrying about the future. He attempted a smile. "Besides, having read what that article says about me, you've probably learned all your dubious sexual habits from me in the first place. If I deny being in a relationship with you, I'm just going to look like your pimp."

It worked to a degree. Al gave a small laugh. "Actually, you may have a point there."

But the smiles faded quickly. Whatever they said, they all still knew that Laurie was bothered. More than bothered—terrified. After a moment, James spoke, however.

"The thing is," he said, slowly, "the university can't do anything to you. As Al says, you've been outright accused of nothing illegal. It's all just innuendo. And we're twenty-five, for god's sake. Trying to prove that you'd done something to us ten years ago or more, even if you had, would be ridiculous, and there's no one who's going to bother. The police won't, and we're not going to. Mum's hardly going to try. In fact, if anyone did claim you'd touched either of us inappropriately, the fact that your boyfriend's mother would stand up in any court and defend you is a pretty strong backing. The whole thing's insulting, and it's fucking scary that people can just go and write that sort of shit—but it's not going to affect your job."

"I guess," Laurie said. He looked at James curiously. When had his boyfriend worked all of this out?

James hadn't finished. He went on: "As to the other stuff...even if you *were* having sex with your students, they'd be of age so the law wouldn't care. It would probably be enough to get you sacked, but as you're not doing it, that's kind of irrelevant."

"The uni doesn't know that, though," Laurie said gloomily.

"Mm. Unless it can prove you are doing it, though...it hasn't got a leg to stand on," James said. "If universities can be said to have legs, that is."

"You know, James has a point," Al said, sounding more hopeful than he had done at any point so far.

"No need to sound so surprised," James retorted. "The point is, Laurie's done nothing wrong. He's going to have to put up with the social media stuff, but his job isn't in jeopardy. In fact, the uni would be in trouble if they tried to go after you for something so nebulous. What has the paper said, really? 'This man's having a relationship with two other men, both of whom he's known for a long time.' God, the horror."

"Jamie," said Al, his voice tinged with awe, "you're on top form tonight."

"Thank you," added Laurie, quietly.

James ignored Laurie, looking at Al. "Suppose you think you've been the only one looking online, do you?" he asked. "Some of us have been doing something other than looking at Twitter." Laurie winced—that was presumably a swipe at him as well as Al. "This isn't school. No one's under age, so there's not the same 'guilty until proven innocent' vibe. Laurie doesn't have to answer anything." He sighed. "Of course, that doesn't mean no one's going to ask," he admitted. "It's not going to be much fun. But the university can't do anything, even if they want to—and none of us are doing anything we need to be ashamed of. You were right—Laurie's life would be a lot easier if he said he was just dating me. But I'm bloody glad he's not going to do that. It's no one's fucking business what—or *who*—he's doing. To put it another way"—James added, with a faint smile—"our fucking business is no one else's fucking business."

That surprised a more genuine laugh out of Al, and even Laurie smiled.

"Jamie, Jamie, Jamie," Al said, shaking his head before leaning forward to give James a quick kiss, "you will never cease to amaze me."

"Nor me."

Laurie put his arms tightly round James, stunned by how much further James had managed to see through the situation than Laurie had himself. You would have thought that Laurie might have been able to work all of that out for himself. As it was, he had apparently been spending the last forty-eight hours feeling humiliated, guilty, and ashamed and doing nothing useful in the slightest. Whereas James...

Laurie thought of the forlorn figure he had seen the moment he walked into the flat. Who would have thought that James had managed to work so much out? If anyone should have known not to underestimate James, it should have been Laurie. But yet again, he had misjudged his boyfriend. He'd been doing that for far too long. A twinge of guilt ran through him. James was yet again proving how much too good for him he was. Laurie tried to push the thought to the back of his head: time enough to worry about that later. What mattered now was showing James his appreciation.

"Thank you," he said again. "You're amazing. And right. I'm being pathetic. Your mum told me so, pretty much—"

"Said she would," interrupted Al. He caught Laurie's expression. "Erm, not the 'being pathetic', but the 'telling you what was what' bit," he explained, hastily.

"Yes, well," said Laurie, feeling his own behaviour didn't leave him in a position to criticise others, "the point is.... Oh god, James, thank you. I've been dreading work on Monday—and yes, Al, before you comment, I know it's been pathetic that I ran away and hid the last couple of days..."

"I said nothing," said Al.

"Well, so." Laurie looked at James particularly as he said the next line. "I've got the weekend to try and make things up to you a bit," he said. "But thank you, Jamie." He kissed James carefully, hesitantly, on the lips, wondering whether his boyfriend would push him away. But James did no such thing, responding as fervently as he always had.

"God, I'd better put the ice cream in the freezer," Al said, jerking back to reality, and breaking a bit of the tension. The other two looked at him. "What?" he asked. "I bought ice cream. I'm a girl. Emotional upset—reach for the ice cream. Now things are looking a bit better, it's all good. Celebration—reach for the ice cream. But it'll be better if it hasn't melted." He stood up. "And before either of you say it, yes, I know that was an obnoxious sexist statement unworthy of me. We still have ice cream, though."

James and Laurie looked at each other and grinned as Al dealt with his shopping. And Laurie put the worst of his doubts to the back of his mind.

For the moment.

Chapter Seven

AL

James was working the next afternoon—a couple of lessons between 4:00 p.m. and 6.30 p.m. for two long-term students of his, meaning he'd be home around seven o'clock or a little after. Whilst he'd missed work on the Thursday, feeling, as he'd put it to Al, as if he'd drunk himself stupid, he had gone in on Friday between 11:00 a.m. and 5:00 p.m. When, between getting home from the wine shop and heading out for ice cream, Al had tentatively asked him how it had been, James hadn't pretended to misunderstand him.

"Okay. None of the students know, nor the people who came through the shop. And Adam—he's the one who shoved the paper in my face— just said 'All right?' and when I said 'Yeah' he left it at that. There's been looks, of course, from the others, but no one's said anything much."

A Saturday afternoon wasn't likely to be too problematic. James would be teaching for a couple of hours and then coming home; he wasn't liable to run into too many people wanting to comment volubly on his private life. James, in fact, thought Al, was likely to have a considerably better afternoon than Al was anticipating. Al had been gearing himself up to speak to Laurie alone, in a conversation which wasn't going to end happily—at least not for Al himself.

Shortly after James had gone out, Laurie disappeared into the kitchen. Al followed him, to find Laurie fiddling around with the last of the lunch ingredients, putting things away and drying up a few plates. They'd had a picnic-type meal—bread, cheese, tomatoes, cucumber, olives. The usual sorts of things. Laurie turned when he realised he had company and smiled at Al.

"Hey, Al. Please don't tell me you've come to cook something for tonight. I'm not sure I'd live through the shock. I know James is out, but I can probably throw something together later, or we can wait until he's home and hope for the best. It feels like taking advantage, but he really does love cooking, you know."

"Actually, I'm glad James is out," Al said. "And no, I didn't come in here to cook. I wanted to talk to you." He paused. "No," he said, at length, "I didn't, not like this. But I need to." He turned and poured himself a tumbler of whiskey. "I know it's 4:00 p.m.," he said, trying to beat Laurie's comment, "but I need it. Want one?"

"It sounds like I might," Laurie said, his voice suddenly serious.

Al poured another and shoved it across.

"It's about James."

"I thought it might be."

Al took a swig of his drink to fortify himself. "Don't leave him again, Laurie," he begged. "Please. You don't know how much James loves you."

"Al..." Laurie began.

Al held up his hand. "Hear me out. I know there was all that crap in the paper, and I know that's bloody horrible to deal with. But that's nothing to do with James. That's due to me. And I really don't need to be in the equation at all. You know I don't. You said I can stay, and I appreciate it, but I don't have to be here. If I'm not here, you and James can have a...y'know, normal relationship. Be a couple, like everybody else. Not something fucking weird with people judging; and no newspapers poking into things that are none of their business."

"But—"

"You maybe don't want to get me to leave because it might upset James," Al ploughed on, determined to get it all out before his willpower could fade, "but he doesn't have to know." He leaned forward and touched Laurie's hand for a second. "Just tell me, if you need to. I won't make a big deal out of it, and I can sort something out. There'll be a film which needs me to be in Scotland to direct, or—or even America, if that'd help. I mean, I've got family out there, after all." Parents he hadn't talked to in years, but Al wasn't sure how much Laurie knew about that. "And James knows I'd go anywhere for a film if I thought it needed it. It doesn't have to be a problem. I can find a reason to be out there. To stay out there, once I'm gone. It can be one of those things. A natural progression."

He tried not to think about moving away. In a life which had been anything but stable, in so many ways, the one thing—except James—which had remained consistent for Al was his home. He'd always lived in London: always lived in this area, more or less. His roots went deep. But Laurie didn't need to know that. For all Laurie knew, Al was as blasé about his home as he was about most other things. Most things except his lovers and his home. Both of which he was potentially on the point of losing. Al swallowed down that thought, too, ignoring the way his stomach felt like he'd plunged off a large cliff unexpectedly.

"It's not the only solution, you know," Laurie said, drinking his whiskey with a determination worthy of a better cause. "It's not the best solution, really."

"I know the paper printed all sorts of lies about you, but if I'm not here then that wouldn't happen."

"But it didn't get it wrong," Laurie said quietly.

"What?"

Laurie drained his glass and held it out for Al to refill. Al did so, almost automatically.

"Sounds like you've been doing a lot of thinking over the last couple of days," Laurie said. "So have I. What hurt about the paper wasn't that it printed a lot of lies about me, but that it printed the truth."

"Don't be ridiculous," Al said, disbelievingly.

Laurie regarded him steadily. "You're asking me to stay for James. You know James. You know what an amazing musician and teacher he is, but even more so, what a bloody wonderful person he is. Caring, generous, fun. And what are you offering him? Me?" His voice was full of self-disgust as he went on. "A creep who did indeed wank over an eighteen-year-old boy, and who now gets a hard-on for dominating someone much younger and smaller about to the point that I've bruised him and made him cry in the past. Is that really what you want for James, Al? Do you really think that's the best he can do?"

There was the sound of breaking glass at Al's feet, and he jumped, staring down. His whiskey glass lay shattered where his hand must have let go of it in his shock at Laurie's words.

"Jesus Christ, Laurie, is that seriously how you see yourself?"

Al ignored the broken tumbler, considering it the least of his problems right now. Listening to Laurie describe the three of them that way... It was true, Al knew, that Laurie had fallen for James when the younger man was eighteen. But despite the fact that eighteen was the age of adulthood, and there could have been few complaints about such a relationship, he hadn't done anything about it. Even when James had made a pass at Laurie almost a year later, Laurie had turned him down, based mostly on his very awareness of the age gap. In fact, it had taken another three years for Laurie to acknowledge his feelings out loud and actually touch James himself in any sexual fashion.

As to the other part... Yes, Al was younger than Laurie—and smaller. But suggesting that anything Laurie did with him was against his will was ridiculous. Al was a more than willing participant, desperate to submit to Laurie as often and as much as he wanted. If there had been tears—and yes, there had, at times—it had been because Al had felt so much, so deeply. It had touched something inside him that practically nothing else in his life had reached. The moments had been precious. As to the bruises... Al flushed, remembering the occasions on which he'd run his fingers over those same bruises, wanking till he came at the memory of how he'd received them. God, he lived for the moments when Laurie and James between them dominated him till he barely knew his own name.

Laurie turned away from him, leaning heavily on the kitchen side. "Truth hurts when you look at it, doesn't it? It's not much fun facing your own reflection."

"But that's not—"

"Yes. It is." Laurie looked over his shoulder to give Al a mirthless smile and tossed back half of the second tumblerful of whiskey. "And a coward, who runs away when faced with things he can't cope with. When James kissed me, that first time. When the papers printed—that. Then there's the time you don't know about—the fact that I might have been able to stop you being raped last year and I didn't because I was too fucking cowardly."

"What the fuck?" Al stared at him at his words, frowning. His rape the previous year was one of those things that they all knew about, of course, but rarely spoke of. And certainly not like this. "Don't be stupid, Laurie. You weren't there."

"Oh," Laurie said, the self-loathing clear in his voice, "but I was there a couple of weeks earlier when I overheard someone making threats about you. I never told you that, did I? I bet James hasn't mentioned it, either, has he?"

Al looked around for his own whiskey and realised that it was in pieces on the floor. He was tempted to swig straight from the bottle. Last year's attack had devastated his life, though out of the ashes of what had been had come something better... At least, he'd thought so until now, when the new life was lying in pieces, much like the whiskey glass.

"No," he said at last. "No, he hasn't." Laurie had known? Or known something, at any rate. And not said a word, either before—or even afterwards? Not even told Al about it? "W-why didn't you?" he asked, shaken.

Laurie shrugged. "Too cowardly," he said.

Al kicked the glass shards in an unexpected burst of fury, listening to them tinkle and crack beneath his unshod foot. "No, Laurie, that's no sort of fucking answer. What the bloody hell went on? And why the fuck did no one think to tell me?" He wasn't sure whether he was actually shaking; he sure as heck felt as if he was.

Laurie finished the second glass of whiskey. He'd be really bloody pissed soon, after getting through that much alcohol in such a swift space of time, Al thought absently. He found it slightly hard to care right now.

"I was out with the department. One of my students... I caught your name. Homophobic threats. Saying you were ripe for a punching. I—er—challenged him about it."

"Why didn't you tell me?" Al asked, his voice low.

"I...just..." Laurie sounded so horribly unhappy. Al half felt sorry for him, but damn it, Al was the one who'd been beaten up and raped. If Laurie could have done anything that would have stopped it... "I didn't take it seriously, not really. I just thought he was—drunk and being a wanker. Plus," Laurie added, ashamedly, "I said something I shouldn't have. Could've risked my job. Didn't want to admit to it." He turned round and looked at Al, and Al was shocked at his appearance. Laurie had rubbed the tears from his eyes before turning, but it was clear they had been there. His face was pale and drawn, with an expression of utter despair on it. He looked twenty years older than Al, not ten. "Still think I'm what James deserves, Al?"

"James knew about this," Al said. It wasn't a question.

"Not till afterwards," Laurie said quickly. "Afterwards, he could see I was—well, hiding something. I told him then."

"But not me."

"No." Laurie made an apologetic gesture with his hands. "It was a bit late by then."

"Yes. Yes, it was." It was Al's turn to look away, to blink back tears. Something occurred to him. "What did you say? That made you worry about your job?"

"Doesn't matter. Not important enough to have risked your safety," Laurie said bleakly.

"I have the right to know, don't you think?"

"I made a stupid threat. Something I shouldn't have said."

"What?"

"Asked him whether he valued the use of his arms," said Laurie briefly.

Al paused, his attention suddenly drawn. Waking up to what Laurie was actually telling him, beneath the layers of self-recrimination. "Because he…" He trailed off.

"Was saying something I didn't appreciate, pretty much. Yes."

"About me."

Laurie gave a little mournful laugh. "Even I don't go about making threats for no reason, Al." He bit his lip, whilst Al tried to visualise Laurie making threats at *all*. It was not an easy thing to imagine in Al's quiet, reserved boyfriend. "I swear to god I didn't think he meant it, though. I was just so angry that he should dare say any fucking thing about you." The drink was kicking in a bit now, loosening Laurie's tongue. "God, if I'd had any idea, I promise I'd have—"

"I know," Al said, cutting across him.

Laurie clearly recollected himself. "Anyway, doesn't matter now. Too fucking late, isn't it?" His voice lowered a pitch or two. "Too fucking late for a lot of things. The point is, James is too good for me. Always has been. I've known it since the beginning, but—well, coward, like I told you. And weak. He offers me something…someone I want more than anything else in the world, and I'm not strong enough to refuse." He held out his glass to Al again. Al took it, but instead of refilling it, he put it on the counter behind him.

"I think you've had enough for the moment," he said.

"Whatever," Laurie said, as if it didn't matter. "And then there's you. Do you know what I thought when James first told me he'd slept with you in the past, Al?" Al shook his head. "I thought, 'How can I compete?' Here's this gorgeous young man, James's best friend, for god's sake. Charming, intelligent, witty. Then there's me. What sort of competition is that?"

"James doesn't love me," Al said quietly.

"Didn't. At least, he didn't know he did at the time. He does now, though." Laurie's eyes were fixed on the whiskey bottle, Al noticed, but he must be finding it hard to see it, the way they were filling with tears again. "You're not the one who needs to be leaving, Al." He repeated it, his voice so quiet it was almost inaudible. "You're not the one who needs to be leaving."

"Laurie, don't do this."

"Both of you, too good for me. I knew from the beginning that you'd leave me in the end." A couple of those tears spilled down Laurie's cheeks, and he wiped them away impatiently. "Fuck, I wanted to do this bit properly. Face it courageously. I've had three and a half years with James and you. So much more than I deserve. Just the thought..." His voice cracked suddenly. "The thought of not seeing—touching—loving... Oh god." He slid to the floor, burying his face in his hands, his shoulders shaking. "Still a coward now, then," he said, his voice wavering and jumping with sobs.

"Laurie, for fuck's sake..." Al moved away from the shattered remains of his whiskey glass, dashing across the room to fall on his knees next to Laurie. "Don't do this."

Laurie was the strong one: the calm, cool, confident one. Bad enough when he'd walked out, but he'd been strong enough to come back—and apologise without reserve, even when he'd had certainly reason enough to be upset. But seeing him sobbing and broken on the kitchen floor was killing Al. Listening to the hitherto completely unexpected levels of self-hatred within Laurie, watching him tear himself apart over his love for James—could it seriously also be for Al?—was awful. How could he possibly think of himself in that way?

"Please, Laurie," Al begged, his hands on Laurie's shoulders, trying to force him to look up and meet his gaze. But Laurie was too well away, unable to do anything but shake in the grip of his weeping, gasping for breath. "Laurie. *Laurie.*" No response but the tears.

Al slapped him.

It shocked them both. Al had simply not known what to do, and with a vague memory of instructions about bringing people out of hysterics, his hand appeared to have acted of its own accord, reaching out and catching Laurie hard—very hard—on the side of the face. Laurie choked and at last looked up. He looked utterly wrecked, and Al felt utterly helpless. And ashamed. He could actually see the imprint of his fingers across Laurie's cheek.

"God, sorry," he apologised quickly. "I didn't mean—"

"No, you were right." Laurie swallowed hard, and rubbed his face with his palms. "I'm being a fucking coward again. I'm sorry. I'll pull myself together." He pressed his lips together tightly for a few seconds.

"We need to discuss how..." His voice shook, and he stopped speaking suddenly, clenching his hands into fists.

"We need to discuss," said Al, his own voice not as steady as it might have been, "how much James and...and...and *I* love you, and how right we are to do so." He still had one hand on Laurie's shoulder, and he felt the way his boyfriend trembled as he spoke. Al exhaled suddenly. "And, apparently, how it seems I'm the one with a penchant for domestic violence. God, I'm so sorry I hit you." He traced the red mark on Laurie's face with a gentle finger, appalled at its vividness.

"I can't do this, Al," Laurie said in a broken whisper. "Help me."

"Don't," said Al, trying to sound cheerful. "Don't, or you'll start me off and then we'll both be bawling. You know what I'm like."

"Al..."

Al wrapped his arms around as much of Laurie as he could. "Don't you know how much we love you, you idiot?"

"I have no idea why."

Al laughed softly. "Oh, that's hard, that is." He kissed Laurie's temple, the only part of him he could easily reach in the position they were currently in. "It's not like I had years of James reciting your perfections to me or anything. Actually, you're right—it's amazing I still managed to fall in love with you after that." He kissed him again, and shifted a little so that he could put a hand on Laurie's face and kiss his mouth. "Fuck, I'm not good at this sort of thing. You're good company, you put up with my shit, you're interesting and intelligent and all that sort of stuff, you're reliable and kind, and I know I can trust you—and on top of all of that, you're bloody fucking hot, and I'm insanely attracted to you."

"After all I've just told you?"

"What, that you've got a hole in your self-esteem the size of a small country and I never knew?" Al asked. He was still in a state of shock at quite how negatively his boyfriend (who had always seemed so self-possessed) regarded himself.

"You know what I mean," Laurie muttered.

"Okay, that you've fancied James since he was eighteen and were careful not to do anything about it because you thought it was inappropriate? Shocking, Laurie. You freaked out about lies in the paper—and they were lies, Laur; don't ever doubt it. I wish you hadn't walked out on us, but I can't blame you."

"And—the other?"

It still made Al feel wobbly inside, thinking about his assault. He'd been thrown for a loop by Laurie's disclosure that he'd known something about it in advance—but actually, thinking about the details of what Laurie had described, would Al have paid much attention to a vague threat in a pub even if he'd heard it himself? Hell, he got enough on Twitter just by existing, especially if he wrote anything about transgender rights, which was a quick way to bring the trolls out in force. As Al's last film had been about the daughter of a transitioning trans man, it was not in the slightest uncommon for this to happen. When it came down to it, what Laurie had in fact told him, which Al had not known before, was that he had risked his reputation, not to mention his job, to defend Al's.

"Thank you," he said quietly, "for defending me." He leaned his head against Laurie's, wondering what was going through his boyfriend's mind. Wondering how much he'd been misunderstanding him all these years they'd known each other. Had Laurie always been so full of self-doubt and self-hatred? He tightened his grip on Laurie, holding him close. "Don't leave us, Laurie. Please. If you honestly want both of us, don't leave us. But I meant it, about me. If—if you need me to go, say." He paused, and listened to himself. Gave a little laugh. "Hell, all we need now is James coming in and offering to leave. Are we all as fucked up as each other?"

For the first time, Laurie relaxed enough to put his arms around Al in turn. "God, I'll start crying again in a minute," he said.

"Don't," said Al, hastily. "I don't think I could take it."

"Sorry. Sorry."

"The stuff you said about—about sex," Al said, needing to get it out. "Us. Fuck, Laurie, don't you have a clue about how much I love submitting to you? How much it turns me on? It's got nothing to do with age, size, whatever." He found his breathing was quickening even talking about it. "I—I choose to. I want to. God, how I want to," he added, half under his breath. "Then, now, any time. If I want it, Laurie...?"

"That's what Gi—" Laurie cut off suddenly.

Al pulled away—another, very different emotion suddenly overwhelming him. "Please tell me that sentence wasn't going where I think it was going," he said urgently. Laurie wouldn't look at him, and Al turned away, feeling his face burning with embarrassment. "Oh god, oh god, please, please tell me that you have not been talking to the nearest thing I have to a mother about...oh bloody hell, Laurie."

"I didn't," Laurie said hastily; "at least, I mean, I didn't say anything. Not really."

"I am never," said Al, "going to be able to go home again." He felt Laurie make a sudden movement at this, and looking up, saw a strange expression on Laurie's face. "What?"

"I was just thinking," Laurie said, cupping Al's face in his hand, "how happy Gillie would be if she heard you say 'home' like that."

"I said...?" Al hadn't thought he could get any more mortified. Apparently, he had been wrong. Not only had he discovered that Laurie had been talking to Gillie about...oh god, their sex life, and specifically Al getting off on kneeling at Laurie's feet... No, he was not going to think about that ever again—*ever again*—but now, apparently Al had just admitted that... "This couldn't get any more embarrassing, could it?"

"She adores you, you know."

Al ducked his head. "As if."

"You're not very good at being loved, Al, are you?" Laurie said softly.

Unexpectedly, tears prickled in Al's eyes. He told himself that it was just that he was tired. Over-emotional. They'd just had a draining conversation—hell, they were still sitting on the kitchen floor, along with the broken remains of a whiskey glass—and his body hadn't caught up with the fact that everything seemed...well, everything was fucked, but somehow not nearly as fucked as he'd thought it was going to be. But Laurie's words, he knew, had hit something deep inside him. Al had never, really, felt that he deserved to be loved. He'd learned to live without it: find pleasure in friendship and sex and films. He was likeable enough—he'd always had plenty of friends, not just James, though no other friends *like* James. But loveable? Hardly.

His earliest memories, his mother's whining voice: *Well, if it wasn't for Alistair, I could...* She'd told him outright once, when he was sixteen, that he'd ruined her life. He'd flipped her the bird and gone out and shagged a woman twice his age; hadn't come back for two nights, spending the second sleeping under a bush in the park. She'd never even commented on his absence, and he didn't think his dad had ever noticed he'd been gone. It had been shortly after that he'd fought depression and damn nearly lost. Would have lost, if it hadn't been for James. And for Gillie and Terry, who had let him stay with them for a fortnight at that point, plus pretty much every weekend for the whole of secondary school—and then instructed him to call their house his own when his parents finally moved abroad, a month after Al started university.

"Al?" Laurie said.

Al realised he had been lost in his brain. "Sorry."

"Nothing to apologise for. Al," Laurie said again, sounding unnaturally nervous, "can I...?"

He put his lips against Al's tentatively, as if expecting Al to push him away. Al blinked the ridiculous tears from his eyes—daft, overemotional idiot—and kissed back, willingly. Laurie needed this as much as he did, Al realised; they both needed reassurance, encouragement, the feeling that... *Well, perhaps neither of them felt as if they deserved it, but still, on some level everyone wanted to be loved, didn't they, really.*

"Shall we take this somewhere more comfortable?" he suggested, suddenly realising how hard the kitchen floor felt underneath him.

"Yes."

But Laurie stayed still after his agreement, and Al realised that it would need to be he who made the first move. Twining his fingers through Laurie's, he got to his feet and gave a little tug. In no world would he ever been able to pull Laurie up if Laurie did not choose to come; the older man was several stone heavier than Al; however, Laurie followed his lead willingly enough. Al led him through into the bedroom and pulled him onto the bed, wrapping himself around his lover and straining towards his mouth.

For a while, they just stayed there, fully clothed, kissing as if they were teenagers, newly involved and in love. It was strange: Al could hardly remember those days. It had mostly been girls back then; and, anyway, in truth he'd never really wanted any emotional relationship, just craved the touch of another human. Laurie and he had started at the wrong end of everything: it had been just sex which had developed into something more, and then something so very much more than Al had ever imagined. Going back to the beginning that they'd never had was...well, rather lovely. After a while, however, Al's hands were somehow inside Laurie's shirt; a little later they were both half-naked. They took their time as they undressed, though, and even when the clothes were all gone, puddled on the floor, the leisurely pace continued, unexpectedly wonderful.

Laurie continued to kiss Al slowly and thoroughly, his hands not aiming directly for every erogenous zone Al had, but skimming lightly over each area of his body in turn, touching it with unfeasibly gentle fingers. Al could never get used to the difference between the size and power of Laurie's hands, and the delicate ways in which he could use them when he chose. He was a conundrum, this large, gentle, dominating lover of his. Ever catlike, Al wanted to purr and stretch under Laurie's touch, settling for running his hands down Laurie's arms, feeling the muscular power within them. He felt warm and aroused, but it was not a desperate, *need it now* arousal, more a feeling of building pleasure which coiled inside him and was slowly unwinding. Laurie was, Al realised, making love to him. Not fucking him; not having sex with him—though both of these things were good, too—making love. Al was too impatient for this sensual teasing to satisfy him on all occasions, but right now it was what both of them needed.

Al rolled over, pushing Laurie under him. It was time to reciprocate; to show Laurie that Al, too, could offer more than a quick fuck. Pulling his mouth away from Laurie's with vague reluctance, he licked a path down Laurie's neck, sucking on the pressure point where he could feel the beat of Laurie's heart. He lay on top of his lover, feeling the heat of their bodies in every point they touched, feeling the hard lump of Laurie's erection against his stomach. Usually, Al would rub against it; this time, he kept his lower half perfectly still, just using his hands and mouth to pleasure Laurie's head and neck and chest, moving warm lips up to nibble Laurie's ear; to push his tongue right inside it.

"You feel so good," he whispered, his hands sliding to touch Laurie's nipples.

Laurie made a little noise—unusual in Al's often-silent lover—and pushed his hips up against Al, increasing the pressure on his cock. And fuck, but that felt good. Al wasn't sure how much longer his good intentions of slowness and patience would last if Laurie did that much more. He was beginning to remember how fantastic it felt to have Laurie inside him, sliding deeper and deeper and...

"Oh god," Al moaned, never good at silence.

"Let me bring you off, Al," Laurie murmured, sliding his hand down and wrapping it around Al's erection.

"Fuck me?"

Laurie shook his head. "Not today. Just—"

"Do us both together then," Al pleaded.

"Mmm. Sounds good."

Laurie reached over for the lube, taking his hand off Al long enough to slick it, and then moving it back to grasp his own and Al's cocks together. It was fortunate that Laurie had such large hands: Laurie had a big cock by any standards, and Al would have struggled to get his fingers round Laurie's and his at the same time. Then Laurie began to move his hand up and down, and Al stopped thinking about any of that. He leaned forward, intending to kiss Laurie some more, but the sensation meant that, instead, he just moaned, open-mouthed, against Laurie's jaw. Laurie's hands. Laurie's gorgeous, gorgeous hand wrapped around Al's cock, pressing it against his own; his other hand resting lightly, possessively, on Al's arse. Al jerked his hips, pushing his erection through Laurie's grasp again and again.

"Laurie, god, I need you so much, please..."

"I've got you." Laurie's deep voice seemed to rumble right through Al's body. "Come on, baby, that's right. So good. Fuck yourself against me."

"Oh please, god, please."

Al's movements were faster, needier. He sucked and licked at Laurie's jaw and neck, murmuring soft, hot words against him. Laurie's hand was speeding up, too; and Laurie's cock was hot and wet with lube. It felt so good; so damn good against Al's own. This was Laurie, his love, making love to him. And that thought was enough to send Al over the edge with a deep cry, shaking and groaning as he lay across Laurie. Laurie kissed his face, wrapping his other arm around Al and holding him close. A few more swift strokes and Laurie himself was coming. Al revelled in the sensation of the warm, sticky come against his stomach, the knowledge that being with him had brought Laurie pleasure as well. It was wonderful, lying there with Laurie after everything which had gone on. Warm, satisfied, comfortable. Al leaned over, pulled the duvet across them, and then lay his head on Laurie's broad chest and shut his eyes.

Chapter Eight

JAMES

James unlocked the front door and walked into an empty living room. No sign of Laurie or Al, which was surprising.

"Hey? Anyone in?" he called.

No response. James walked into the kitchen, to a half-empty bottle of whiskey on the counter with one empty glass behind it. Another tumbler was smashed on the floor, shards of glass covering a disconcertingly large amount of space, with amber liquid clearly visible in little rivulets and pools. Not good. Not good at all. What the hell had been happening whilst James was out of the house? And why was no one in? Shit. James had seen a look in Al's eye that morning which spelt determination, and he had a horrible feeling that Al was intending to have some sort of *talk* with Laurie. Judging by the signs, the talk had not been a positive one. So, where the blazes were either of James's boyfriends? That one might have stormed out, James could believe, however little he wanted to consider it; it seemed surprising, not to mention extremely alarming, that they'd both go.

Fuck. Fuck, fuck, fuck.

James had hoped that things were on the mend; that although there was a lot of work all three of them needed to do on their relationship, they could get through this. Maybe even be stronger at the other side, though even in James's most optimistic moments that seemed a long way off. Broken kitchenware and missing lovers wasn't exactly the best implication, however. Bugger it. Sighing, he turned away and went towards the bedroom. He pushed open the door, intending to have a quick change out of his work clothes before going out on some sort of hunt for his missing boyfriends—god knew where; he'd work on that when he came to it—and pulled up short.

Not out. Apparently not arguing, either. Asleep on his back in the middle of the huge bed lay Laurie, and sprawled across him, looking oddly small against the backdrop of Laurie's broad chest, lay an equally asleep Al. Shutting the door as silently as possible, James leaned against it, taking in this disconcerting view. It was, he had to admit, rather adorable. Laurie's arm was curled protectively around Al, even in his sleep; and Al, his head pillowed on Laurie, looked young, fragile—and, James thought, with a little smile, extremely sexually satisfied. They were both, as far as James could see for the duvet, naked; and the fact that clothes were scattered around the vicinity of the bed suggested that this was indeed the case. Al's cheeks had a hint of pink in them, and his mouth was curved up in a small smile.

As James watched, Laurie blinked and opened his eyes.

"James," he said quietly. "Glad you're home."

James leaned over the bed and kissed him. "You seem to have been reasonably well occupied as it is," he retorted, in a similarly low tone. "Care to tell me what's been going on in the kitchen?"

"Oh." Laurie frowned suddenly. "Shit. Sorry about that."

"Sorry about what?" mumbled Al, his eyes still closed.

"Kitchen," Laurie said succinctly.

"Oh bugger. Sorry, James. Dropped a glass." Al kept his eyes shut but reached out a hand in the direction from which he had heard James's voice and patted at him vaguely. "I'll go and clear it up in a sec."

"You do know you freaked the hell out of me, don't you?" James said, returning to normal tones now both of his lovers were awake. He sat down on the side of the bed. "I came in, and no one seemed to be in, *and* you'd apparently had a fight in the kitchen... What the heck actually happened?"

"Dropped it," said Al again, stretching lazily and finally deigning to open his eyes. "Hey, gorgeous James. Good day?"

"You're changing the subject," James said severely.

"Yes, but very subtly." Al pushed himself up with a hand on Laurie's shoulder and reached over to press his lips to James's. "We got distracted. Sorry."

"So I can see," James said dryly.

"Sorry we scared you," Laurie apologised. "I just crashed out."

"Not surprised, seeing the amount of whiskey that's gone."

"Most of it's on the floor," Laurie said, slightly defensively.

Al snorted. "Most of it's in you." He kissed Laurie's forehead absently. "It was mine that got dropped. It's amazing you could get it up, the amount you drank."

"So Laurie got smashed, you just smashed things, and then you both ended up in bed." James grinned. "Sounds like a good afternoon was had by all. And there I was, teaching a bloke how to play 'Brown Eyed Girl' on the guitar. How the other half live, eh?"

Laurie and Al exchanged a glance, and James's grin faded a bit. Clearly, there had been more going on than he was going to hear about, at least at the moment. However, equally clearly, it seemed to have ended up reasonably well. It was probably better just to let it pass.

"Well," he said at length, "glad it ended up well."

Al smiled the smug smile that James was really rather fond of and leaned across to kiss James again. "It did. It very much did." He stretched. "God, I'm starving. If I clean the kitchen up, will someone else cook? I'd do it, but the aspersions Laurie was casting on my cookery skills earlier were enough to make anyone drop several glasses, and—"

"Al, if you dropped glasses every time one of us made a perfectly accurate comment about your cooking, we'd have none left," James said ruthlessly. "I keep offering to teach you, but you turn me down."

"Yeah, well," said Al, grinning, "I'm not an idiot. If I start being able to cook, you might not make me things."

James rolled his eyes. "It'd serve you right if I made something you don't like, except you like everything. Fine. Vegetable risotto. But you can bloody well vacuum the floor as well as sweeping up the glass. I'm not risking getting shards of glass in my foot cooking for people who can't be arsed to learn."

"Fair enough," Al agreed easily.

"I'll cook, if you like. I ought to do something useful," Laurie offered. There was a half-sad note in his voice as he said that, which made James look at him with slight concern.

"Don't be daft," he said roughly. "You know I'm happy pottering around in the kitchen. Come and keep me company, if you want, otherwise I'll stick some music on and be quite content." He leaned in and gave Laurie another kiss. "But Al's clearing up. He dropped the damn glass. He can deal with the bits."

IT WAS AL who was working the following day. He had a shift at the wine shop on most Sundays, working either 12:00 p.m. to 10:00 p.m. or starting a couple of hours later at 2:00 p.m. This was an early day, so he was in for the long haul. The men's differing shift patterns meant that it was difficult for them to get a day when all three of them were free, which could be frustrating. It would have been nice to do things together as a threesome more often. James made a vow that this needed to be something they prioritised in future—the thought of having long, lazy days with Laurie and Al sounded heavenly. A holiday, too; the three of them had never been on holiday together, though James had been with both Al and Laurie separately on different occasions.

But there was a lot of sorting out to be done before they got to that stage. James was pretty certain that much more had happened between Laurie and Al the previous day than he'd heard about, even over the course of a long and conversational evening. The fact that Laurie had a bruise forming on his cheek, for a start. James had looked at that thoughtfully, but neither of the others mentioned anything about it, and James had decided that discretion was indeed the better part of valour. However, today, James had decided that he and Laurie were going to have to have a few things out together. It seemed Laurie was feeling the same way. James had felt Laurie's eyes on him for a lot of the morning, even when Laurie was theoretically working.

After lunch, however, Laurie still hadn't said anything. The two of them were sitting at either end of the sofa. Laurie had his laptop open, but James was pretty sure he wasn't doing anything useful. He seemed to be staring blankly at the screen a lot of the time. James had a guitar on his lap and was strumming chords idly, but with no great effort. He came to a decision and placed it down. Before he could speak, however, Laurie got in.

"I'm sorry," he said, for about the tenth time. "I know I ought to say something else, but I just don't know what to say." His eyes, when they met James's, were troubled.

"I asked Al to fuck me, the night you left," James said, abruptly. He hadn't meant to say that; had certainly not meant to start with it as an opening gambit, but the words had just come out of his mouth before he could stop himself.

He saw Laurie go very still. "I hurt you very badly, didn't I?" was all his lover said, however.

"Well, what do you think, Laurie?" James demanded. "We've been together coming up to four years, but that's apparently not as important as something some dickhead writes in a paper? You just walked out on me—on us."

"I know. I'm sorry," Laurie said again. He was silent for a second. "About Al," he said gently. "I'm guessing he said no."

"I say 'asked'. More like 'begged'," James said. It was true, but James also knew that he wanted to punish Laurie a little for his rejection. He went back through the evening in his memory; the way he'd clung to Al and pleaded with him. "Very like 'begged', actually," he said; and this time it was embarrassment which led him to admit it. God, he'd been in a state.

Laurie slid across the sofa towards him and pulled him into his arms. "I'm so, so sorry," he whispered. "I wish I could change what I did. Tell me what I can do to try and make things right. Or—I don't know... Maybe there's nothing I can say or do."

James rested his head on Laurie's shoulder, putting his arms around him in turn. "You're here now," he said. His throat felt choked.

"Yes. For what it's worth," Laurie added grimly. "I shouldn't have done it, Jamie. I just— I couldn't think straight. I felt... I can't even tell you how I felt. I was so..." He sighed. "It doesn't matter now."

"I wish you had let me help," James said wistfully. "I wish you'd let me help now."

"You do—you have."

"You need to talk to me, Laurie. Not just keep it all bottled up. I'm your boyfriend. That's what I'm here for. Not just for the good times, not just for the sex. I've been with you nearly four years, for fuck's sake. I'm not just a passing fling. You need to start trusting me."

He felt Laurie's wince; it went right through both of them. "I know," Laurie said quictly. "But you weren't the problem. You never were."

"Al?"

"Hardly." Laurie pulled back a little so that he could look at James. "And talking of Al...?"

"Oh, you were quite right," James admitted. "He wouldn't fuck me. He did everything he could, but not that."

"Worried you'd regret it. Would you have regretted it?" Laurie asked.

"Probably." James swallowed and continued. "I'm not sure I'd regret it now, though," he said, hesitantly. "If—if he—"

The grip around James tightened. Laurie held him very close, saying nothing, until James began to worry that he'd said something unforgivable. Finally, Laurie spoke.

"If it's something you want," he said. "Is it?"

"I—I don't know," James said truthfully. "Maybe? I— It feels weird even to think about it, but—"

"But you are thinking about it." Laurie pressed a kiss to James's head. "There's nothing wrong with that. We're not—it's not like before. We're not a couple, plus Al. We're a threesome." He leaned back, so that he could look at James. "Al still doesn't think that, though, you know," he said. "He...offered to leave again, yesterday. That's what we'd been talking about. That, and—other stuff. Said we could do it so you'd never know I'd thrown him out—or that's what it came down to, in the end."

"And what did you say?"

"Jamie!" Laurie said reproachfully. "Do you think I'd be telling you if I'd said 'Yes, I think that's a fine plan'?"

"Just wondering why Al dropped his glass. He's not usually clumsy."

"No, that's you," said Laurie, with a faint smile.

James felt a wash of colour suffuse his face. He wasn't horrendously clumsy, but he couldn't deny that of the three of them, if someone was going to break something it would be him more often than not.

"Thanks."

"If you must know," Laurie said, "I told him about last year. What I overheard."

"He wouldn't hold you responsible for that," James objected.

"Gave him a bit of a shock, though. You can hardly blame him," Laurie added in a low tone, "after all he went through."

James gave his boyfriend a small shake. "It was not your fault," he said firmly, glaring at him. "I didn't know you were still stewing over that."

Laurie gave a wry smile. "Still stewing over a lot of things, my James," he said. "I don't deserve you, and I know it. I told Al if anyone was leaving, it should be me. It's not you I don't trust; it's not him. It's me. I know I ought to leave you two. I'm the misfit, not Al. And you'd be a good couple."

"Don't you fucking dare," James hissed at this, his fingers digging deep into Laurie's shoulders. "Don't you even fucking think about it." He gave a small laugh. "God, you and Al had one hell of a chat, then, didn't you?"

"Yes." Laurie nodded. "Yes, we did. I think...maybe...we needed to, though. Like we needed to, too, you and me. I think we all did quite a bit of thinking over the days straight after what happened. I know I messed a lot up when I left. I wouldn't blame you if you couldn't forgive me. I don't... I don't have the strength to let you go unless you ask me..."

"I told you," James said, gripping tighter still. Laurie, leaving forever. Even considering it did something unbearable to James; even just the thought. "Don't you fucking dare. Please, Laurie."

Laurie kissed him softly on the lips. "I can't. I love you too much. I'm much too selfish. But Jamie, if you want Al, and if you want him to fuck you... I know he wants to fuck you; that's always been obvious. But if it's what you want, love, I will support you all the way." He ran his hands over James, gently, lovingly. "Anything you want, James, always."

James could feel the love in Laurie's voice trickling through him, warming him, taking away the worst of the coldness which had seeped into his heart when Laurie left. Laurie loved him, just as Al had sworn. Maybe he wasn't perfect; maybe he had run away when he should have stayed. But he had come back, and quickly. And perhaps Laurie was right. Perhaps they had, all three of them, needed to think about things. To understand what it was they had, and what they wanted, and how they worked—how they would go on working—as a triad. Al's relationship with the other two always would be a little different. James could imagine neither himself nor Laurie sleeping with anyone else, whereas it seemed quite natural and right for Al to find other partners. But their relationship was precious, and it seemed as if they had all thoroughly realised this.

"I love you, Laurie," he said, softening into Laurie's embrace; wanting to burrow against the other man until neither was certain where one man ended and the other began. "I love you so much. Don't ever leave me, please. Please."

"I don't ever want to hurt you." Laurie kissed every part of James's face that he could reach, over and over. "James. God, James. Love you so much."

James kissed back, his fingers sliding down to the buttons on Laurie's shirt, unfastening them. He pressed his hands against Laurie's skin and felt himself tremble slightly at the touch. He remembered the first time they'd done this, the way his body had started shaking just at the sensation of Laurie's naked chest against his own. It had mattered so much from the very beginning. It mattered so much still. *Laurie* mattered so much.

Laurie leaned back to strip James's T-shirt from him and then pulled him close against him again. So warm. James's arms slipped round Laurie's back, and he held him tight. Not speaking, not even kissing, just standing there, holding one another as if neither of them could ever let go. Then Laurie's mouth was back on James's neck, sucking and nibbling at it. Still holding tight, he began to slide to his knees in front of James.

"Please?" he asked softly, his fingers hesitant on James's trousers.

"Let me, too?" James asked.

Laurie looked up at him, a little anxious frown on his face. "But you don't—"

"Don't finish that sentence," James said quickly. He knew what Laurie was going to say: that James didn't like giving head. But it wasn't true—not exactly. He didn't have the same passion for it which he'd seen in both of his boyfriends (though heaven knew he was delighted that they both enjoyed it so much) but he enjoyed it occasionally; and he very much enjoyed what it sometimes did to Laurie, in particular. And right now, he needed to feel Laurie fall apart for him, the same way James fell apart for Laurie so often. "I want to."

"James," Laurie breathed, his voice almost reverent. "God, yes."

Laurie unfastened James's trousers and pulled them down, mouthing over James's pants-clothed cock, which was already hardening. James made a little noise in his throat. It would be so easy to stay here, wind his fingers in Laurie's hair, and let him suck his cock until James was undone and coming down Laurie's throat. But James wanted more. He wanted this to be about *them*, about both of them, and their mutual love and attraction. Stepping out of his trousers, and with a distinct reluctance, he stepped away from Laurie, and threaded his fingers through his boyfriend's.

"Come to bed. Let me suck you at the same time you do me," he pleaded.

"Yes."

Laurie wouldn't let go of James as they made their way through. Back on his feet, he wrapped his arms around him, his mouth licking and kissing James's shoulder and neck as his hands trailed over the expanses of James's bare skin. One hand moved further down, stroking James through his dampened pants until James was breathing heavily, half-laughing at Laurie's insistence.

"I need you, Jamie," Laurie whispered.

"Always," James said. His fingers fumbled as he worked on Laurie's belt, unable to concentrate properly. "God, these— Laurie…"

Laurie laughed softly, helping James with the buckle, and shrugging himself out of his trousers and pants in one go. And Laurie's cock was bloody amazing, James thought, looking at it as if for the first time again. His boyfriend was beautiful, and maybe—maybe he'd taken that for granted a little bit. He wanted to fling himself at Laurie's feet and promise that he'd never take the older man for granted, if only he'd stay. But the words wouldn't come, and James found he was just the slightest bit shy, suddenly. Ridiculous—as if he and Laurie hadn't done everything under the sun together at some point in their relationship. But James wanted to get it right; he wanted to get it *so* right, and that added an unexpected pressure that James wasn't used to feeling.

"James. Please. Let me…"

Laurie pushed James onto the bed and kissed him with a desperation which took away some of James's nerves. Laurie wanted this. He wanted James. Yes, he'd left—but he'd come back. He'd come back, and James shouldn't doubt…mustn't doubt. He melted into Laurie's kisses—no, not melted, combusted with the heat and passion. Fuck, he… His hand went to Laurie's cock, stroking the long length of him, and Laurie thrust into his grip.

"You know I love your hands, Jamie," Laurie said quietly, and James knew what he meant: he was suggesting that James brought him off this way, as James had done many times before.

"No," James said. He remembered the tone of voice in which Laurie had said "God, yes" when James had asked to go down on him. "Turn around. Let me get my mouth around you. If I can," he added, with a small smile. Laurie's cock was sometimes a challenge in that regard, though James certainly wasn't complaining about its size.

Laurie twisted so that he and James were lying in the sixty-nine position. "I was going to take my time," he murmured, sliding his fingers beneath the waistband of James's underwear and pushing it down, "but I can't. I can't."

James said nothing in return, instead lowering his mouth and licking a stripe down the underside of Laurie's cock. Laurie gave a decadent moan, more reminiscent of Al than of James's more reserved lover; and James wondered why he didn't do this more often.

"Oh," he murmured in response, "you like that?"

"I like...? Yeah, James."

But James's name was cut off in a harsh breath as James repeated the action before sliding his tongue round the head of Laurie's cock in a smooth, sensual motion. Laurie muttered an expletive under his breath and licked a path down the side of James's prick in turn. This time it was James breathing heavily, but he continued the motion of his tongue, sucking the whole tip of Laurie's cock into his mouth and closing his lips around it. Laurie's hips twitched, as if he was trying hard not to thrust into James's mouth...and maybe James did understand why his boyfriends enjoyed doing this so much, because Laurie was so bloody reactive as James began to suck him with more intent. With his mouth full of James's prick, he couldn't form words, but there were constant sounds of need and desire slipping from Laurie's mouth, and fuck, but it was hot hearing Laurie like this. Saliva slid from James's mouth, slicking Laurie and dripping down onto his balls. At the same time, James could feel the heat of Laurie's lips, the slide of Laurie's tongue around him. It was hard to keep his concentration with Laurie working him over like this, but he knew that Laurie's technique was sloppier than usual—that his boyfriend was having the exact same problem because of what James was doing to him. James went down further, deep throating Laurie, and Laurie groaned loudly, his mouth slipping off, replaced by his hand as he cried out, helpless in the throes of James's ministrations.

"Fuck, Jamie. Please. God. Yes."

James gave a throaty chuckle, loving the way it sent tremors through Laurie as he did so. Laurie returned to licking James, but gently, as if he did not trust himself to take James in further; as if his control was too fragile to cope with more. His hand slid up and down James's shaft, already wet from Laurie's tongue, and oh *god,* that felt good. But James was going to make Laurie fall apart, fully and totally—make his lover realise that he must not, could not, leave. That he belonged here, with James. James lengthened his throat, swallowing Laurie down and listening to his boyfriend whisper desperate words of need, becoming more and more broken as Laurie came closer to the edge. The motions on James's own cock were jerky and uncoordinated, which James found far more satisfying than the most technically talented efforts might be, speaking as it did of Laurie's arousal. Laurie jolted and came, salt-musk-bitter seed filling James's mouth and forcing him to move back to breathe and swallow around it.

"God, James, *Jamie...*" Laurie groaned.

"Mm-hm," James said, smiling, his head resting on Laurie's thigh.

"Fuck, you..." Laurie took a few deep, desperate breaths, and then turned his attention to James with full force, as if determined to give as much as he'd received.

It didn't take long. Laurie knew how to take James apart, and he did so with loving ruthlessness until it was James reduced to wordless incoherence under him. Afterwards, they lay together.

"I love you so much," Laurie said quietly. "Please, James, don't doubt that."

"Shh." James pressed a kiss to the corner of Laurie's mouth. "We've talked. We've fucked. Let's just lie here. Enjoy the afterglow. I feel good. Do you feel good?"

Laurie gave a little laugh. "As if you need to ask." His arms closed around James, holding him close. "No more talking. I've got it. Love you, Jamie."

"Love you too." But then, James's love had never been in doubt.

Chapter Nine

Laurie

Laurie was glad that Gillie had offered to meet him for breakfast on Monday. He still had half an urge to cut and run—to phone in sick to the university once more, or worse, just proffer his resignation and never go back. James had woken with him that morning, kissing him and wishing him good luck—practically a sign of the impending apocalypse, since James emphatically did not do mornings as a general rule. Laurie had secretly wondered whether James could read his mind and knew he was considering bottling out again. Though looking back over his recent behaviour with a jaundiced eye, it would hardly be surprising. It wasn't as if Laurie had managed to do anything except run away, of late.

"Hi Gillie," he greeted his best friend in the cafe she'd suggested. "Thanks for this."

"Glad to. How are you?" Gillie asked, her tone meaningful.

Laurie leaned down and gave her a kiss before going to order and then sitting down. "*We're* good. I think," he said. "Sorry for running out on you, but—"

"I'm not. I was delighted," Gillie interrupted.

"I know. I appreciate you not telling me to get my head out of my arse and sort myself out. You must have been tempted."

"Darling. You needed a bit of time and space. I knew that." She took a sudden sharp look at him, before frowning. "What have you done to your face?"

"My...?" Laurie put one hand up. Oh, bloody hell, the bruise from where Al had hit him. Ye gods, that was just what he needed to make himself look like a dubious character. And how was he going to explain that one?

"It looks like someone hit you," Gillie said, her expression worried.

"Not that I didn't deserve it," Laurie said ruefully, "but it wasn't like that." He felt himself going pink. "I...um...had a bit of a meltdown. Al provided the suggested cure for hysterics." He gave a reminiscent smile; in retrospect, Al's look of absolute horror when he realised what he'd done was rather amusing. "He was mortified afterwards."

"*Al hit you?*"

"Mm. He's a lot stronger than he looks, too." Laurie rubbed his cheek thoughtfully. "It worked, though. It's just a pity about the timing—the last thing I need is looking like I get into brawls as well."

"Hysterics, lovely?" Gillie asked softly.

"Can we...not?" Laurie begged. "Humiliating enough at the time. I'd rather not relive it. But please don't be angry with Al. He did nothing wrong. I think he panicked, but it was what I needed."

"Poor Al." Gillie raised her own hand and touched the bruise gently. "Poor Laurie. Okay, I won't say any more. As long as you're all all right."

"Thanks." Laurie smiled at her. "We're all doing okay. I promise you, I've apologised profusely to your sons... Oh god, I hope no one overheard that, they'd have a field day..." Gillie let out a little snort of laughter which was reminiscent of her son—both her sons, Laurie thought with rueful amusement—at this. "And neither of them have bailed on their jobs, so I'd better get a grip and deal with my end of things. Damned if I'm going to be the only one who fucks up *again*."

The waitress brought across his coffee and his bacon baguette, and he thanked her. Gillie looked at him.

"The university—" she began.

"Can't do anything, legally, to me, I know," Laurie finished. "James pointed it out, in long and eloquent detail." James's mother's mouth curved a little in a smile at this. "At least, so long as none of the students claim I've done anything to them."

"Why would they?"

"Why would someone write that article in the first place?" Laurie asked grimly. "There are some pretty awful people out there, Gill."

"Not that many," said Gillie sturdily.

"It's going to be there, though, isn't it? All the time, from now on. Students will come into the uni knowing me as the lecturer who's probably out to molest them," Laurie said quietly. "The ones there will be looking at me, wondering. I'm never going to be comfortable being a personal tutor again—not having some kid of eighteen in my office alone with me. And they're going to run in the opposite direction rather than put themselves in that position. It doesn't matter whether it's true or not, there's always the chance that it might be. Any kid with any sense would keep well away. And that's just the students themselves. Their parents...the press... What am I supposed to say if anyone asks me about it? Or even if they say anything? Ignore it?"

"If you can. Engaging at all is probably a bad plan." Gillie ran her fingers through her already messy red hair. "Goodness, I don't know. I'm sitting here giving advice like I have the faintest idea what I'm talking about when I haven't a blessed clue! On the other hand"— she smiled, but it was not her usual gentle smile—"if people start saying slanderous things about my son, they may live to regret it. Don't worry, Laurie, I won't bring you into any conversations in *that* sense that I don't need to, but I doubt I'll be able to help myself. There's been... Well, I've heard a little. But it's generally been about how awful it is that papers can publish anything they want. I don't think it will be as bad as you worry it will, lovely."

"Mm." Laurie forced a smile. "Well. I hope you're right."

He was definitely glad to have support. Walking onto the university campus took much more strength even than he had anticipated. Gillie saw him tense up and slipped her arm through his.

"We can do this. Laurie, you're not alone."

Laurie gave a little snort, half amusement, half anxiety. "That's the problem, isn't it?"

Gillie looked up at him. "Would you rather be?"

Oh. *Oh.* And that put things into perspective. Because, of course, Laurie would rather have James and Al and be facing this situation than be alone and untroubled. He turned and gave her an impulsive hug.

"No," he admitted softly. "You know I wouldn't. Thanks, Gillie. I needed that reminder. They're worth it, your boys. My boys. My *men*," he corrected himself hastily. "My blokes. Whatever." He took a deep breath. "Even if the worst happens. They're worth it."

"Laurie," Gillie said, "I love you. Go out and do it, honey."

"Yes," Laurie agreed. "I will."

His fears were realised as he walked into the Film Studies Department, however. Gerald, the Head of Department, called out to him as he arrived.

"Ah, Laurie." There was a stiff awkwardness in his manner, and Laurie winced internally.

"Hello, Gerald."

"I just—" Gerald coughed, a little embarrassed noise. "—wanted to check that you were quite all right. You know, with—everything."

"Thank you," said Laurie non-committally.

"I...er," Gerald pressed on, "if you wanted to talk to anyone about... anything...there is always...well, obviously, my door is always open" — an incorrect claim: it was usually closed, in Laurie's experience—"but there is Jenny, the Equality and Diversity Manager and...well, I don't know whether there is anything you feel that you might share with the university?"

"No," Laurie said, understanding why people wanted the floor to open up and eat them. If it hadn't been for the fact that Gerald looked almost as uncomfortable as Laurie felt, it would have been worse still. "I mean, thank you, but—everything is quite fine."

"Um, right. Well..." Gerald was stammering onto another sentence when there was a fortunate interruption.

"Laurie. I was looking for you." A familiar female voice came from a little way down the corridor, and Laurie gave Gerald an apologetic smile as he turned to face Annabel, a sixty-something lecturer who was also a good friend of his. He'd known her since his own university days, and she'd supervised his PhD.

"Hi Annabel. Did you need me?"

"Yes." Annabel nodded at the Head of Department. "Hello, Gerald. Had you finished talking to Laurie?"

"Erm, yes. Yes, of course." Gerald, looking pink and discomfited, scuttled back into his office with relieved rapidity.

Laurie, despite his liking for Annabel, felt his heart sink a little. Did another person want to discuss his personal life? Annabel gave him a sympathetic smile.

"Don't worry," she said, her eyes amused. "I haven't any intention of asking any questions. I just thought that you—and Gerald, to be quite honest—needed rescuing. Come along to your office. With any luck, you'll be safer there."

"Annabel," Laurie said gratefully, "you are a lifesaver. Thank you."

"Any time. This is not something," Annabel said, in her precise tones, "which I have much experience in, but I imagine you could do with a little time to yourself."

"Life," said Laurie fervently, "saver."

She gave him a little nod and disappeared into her own office, leaving Laurie to find his way to his and slip in with a sense of relief. The conversation with Gerald had been awkward and hideously embarrassing, but it was clear that there was no immediate threat to Laurie's job from the university establishment, which was an undoubted relief. And Annabel's interruption had been both welcome and thoughtful—not to mention, Laurie knew, her way of showing her support for Laurie. Of course, everything that happened so far showed that he had been right to think that everyone in the entire department knew what had been written about him. Laurie hated the thought, but it was probably inevitable. And given that was the case, so far, he supposed, so good.

He got half an hour of peace (his first lecture wasn't until 11:00 a.m., but he had plenty of catching up in terms of other work to get on with) before there was a knock at his door.

"Hello?" he said wearily, still holding the printout on which he'd been scribbling notes, but turning his chair towards the door.

"Laurie?" A blonde head peered round at him.

"Hi, Polly."

Laurie smiled at her. He was in demand today, it seemed—rather as he'd feared—but Polly was his closest friend in the department, so he was not ungrateful to see her.

"Can I come in?"

"Be my guest." He flashed her a look as she entered and shut the door behind her. "If you think it's safe."

"Yes, I gathered it was a bit like that." She patted him on the shoulder as she sat down. "But I'm too old and the wrong gender, apparently. How are you, Laurie? Really?"

"Humiliated. Worried." Laurie looked straight at Polly. "And please don't pass that on. If anyone asks you, I'm doing just fine. No problems. No comment because there's nothing worth commenting on."

"And how's Al? Presuming you know," Polly added. "I'm making no assumptions."

"Mm, yes, you *would* ask that." Laurie raised an eyebrow at her. He'd gathered, from something she'd said on an evening out together over a year ago, that she was one of the people who had slept with Al in the past. "He's doing well, considering. Better than I have been, anyway."

"It's a lot of nonsense. Everybody knows that," Polly said robustly. Then, curiously, "How did you know, incidentally—about me and Al?"

Laurie absent-mindedly drew a snail on the side of the paper in front of him. "He didn't tell me, if that's what you're asking." A shrug. "Something in the way you looked, when you once made a comment saying he wasn't gay." He gave her a rueful smile. "I knew how you knew, if you get me. Because, as you and the rest of the world are now aware, I've known him a very long time. It's given me a certain level of insight. But it's nice to know there's someone in the department who knows for certain he's not like the paper claimed."

"Oh, I'm not the only one," Polly assured him, eyes amused. "The SCR was interesting on Thursday, and the Film Studies Department meeting even more so on Friday morning."

Laurie groaned, running a hand through his hair. "Oh, bloody hell, how many of the department has he slept with? Do I even want to know?"

Polly laughed. She had a rich, deep laugh which was highly contagious. Laurie found himself grinning, despite his genuine mortification. "Well, for certain, at least three—that is, presuming that some aspects of the newspaper report were accurate?" She looked at him inquiringly.

"Very delicately put, Poll," Laurie said admiringly. "And yes, that bit at any rate was correct."

"Now that, I would never have guessed."

"Polly, can we please skip over the whole thing where we've slept with the same bloke?" Laurie pleaded.

Strangely, though, his heart was lighter than it had been for a while. Talking to Polly about the entire kerfuffle... Laurie could see, suddenly, that there were amusing elements to it, not least that whilst his friends in the department had known he was gay, he was pretty sure that he would otherwise have been fairly low down their list on the possibilities of people with scandalous personal lives. Ye gods, wouldn't it have been more convenient if it were true? But Laurie wouldn't give up James or Al unless he had to. This whole situation had taught him that much, at least.

The giggle which came from Polly in response was unexpected and very clearly genuine. "Sorry," she apologised, trying to stop herself from further laughter. "I'd never thought of it like that. Oh god, Laurie. Sorry. If it were anyone but Al..."

"Story of my bloody life," Laurie assured her, unable not to smile in response. "Trust me."

"But how... Sorry, I shouldn't ask," Polly apologised.

"He's James's—that's my boyfriend—rather, my original boyfriend," Laurie corrected himself. "Anyway, he's James's best friend. I've known them both—well, you know the rest of that sentence." It was strange, realising that everyone he met knew things about him which he'd kept private for years. Strange, and uncomfortable, even when it was someone he liked as much as Polly.

"Look," Polly pointed out, "I'm really very fond of my best friend too, but I'm not having sex with her. And I wouldn't be, even if she was a him. If you follow me."

Laurie had two options: he could either shut down and say nothing further, just as he had decided to do as a general rule if anyone were to ask personal questions of this sort of nature, or he could be blunt. Unexpectedly, to himself at least, he chose bluntness.

"Your best friend isn't Al."

Laurie and Polly exchanged a long look after he said this, and an expression of amusement reluctantly spread over Polly's face.

"You win," she said, her eyes dancing.

"Well, I think I do," Laurie said, with a smile. "I mean—I didn't mean to fall in love with him, you know, but—"

"Oh." Polly stilled after that one syllable. "Oh. I mean, I guess, I suppose..."

"I said that out loud, didn't I?" Laurie said, jerking back to himself suddenly in the force of Polly's reaction. "Damn."

"No, not at all," Polly said hastily. "It's just—"

"Me and Al as a thought was bad enough. My being in love with Al is a step too far."

"It's lovely," Polly said, falling over herself in nervous embarrassment. "It's—it's just—"

It was extremely helpful that she was so embarrassed: it helped him get over his own discomposure. This was the first time Laurie had actually told anyone else that he was in love with Al. Apart from Al himself, of course—and he didn't precisely go out of his way to tell Al, come to think of it—though it wasn't as if Al wasn't aware of the fact. But even when they'd told Gillie they were together, they'd concentrated on the fact that they *were* together and let their feelings for each other be presumed from that.

"Mm?" he said with a smile.

Polly shook herself, glanced round to check the door was shut, and then squealed in a tone of voice entirely inappropriate for a senior lecturer, "You're *in love with Al Hitchins!*" She grinned at him, her expression still a little embarrassed. "Sorry, Laurie, but that's the most scandalous thing I've heard in ages! And I'm a forty-one-year-old woman with a nose for gossip. Fantastic, but—"

"Polly, there's just been an article outing me as living with two men—two much younger men, whom according to the article I possibly corrupted in their early teens or worse—and suggesting I molest my students. And you're not shocked by any of that, but by the fact that I happen to be in love with my boyfriends?" Laurie shook his head. "You need to get your priorities right, woman."

She frowned suddenly. "That article was unforgivable. I'm so sorry. And furious on your behalf. Which is, by the way, the feeling of most of the department—because yes, of course everyone's been talking about it. I'm not going to lie." Her eyes sparkled a little. "But Al Hitchins, that's just...wow!" Laurie blushed. He could feel the colour seeping all over his face and even his ears. "But don't you mind that he..." Polly broke off, but Laurie knew where the sentence was going.

He sighed. "I'm in love with Al Hitchins. Not some imaginary version of him. No, I don't care in the slightest. I'd care if James slept with other people, because it would mean something was wrong between us. I'd care if Al stopped. It would mean there was something very, very wrong with him."

"Laurie Rose, you are a dark horse," Polly announced.

He gave her an ironical look. "If only I still were, Polly. If only I still were..."

But the conversation, nevertheless, cheered him up. Whilst it was mortifying to know that the department had, indeed, been buzzing with gossip about him—and about Al, who was well known within it also—it was good to know that his colleagues were on his side, more or less. As well as working with Laurie, many of the lecturers had taught Al during his university days. Al had also come in to speak to students on various occasions, so was known to more recent members of staff, too (not that it had been so very long since he had been there, mind you). He was generally liked, which was not surprising as Al was easily likeable. Laurie got through the day without anyone else specifically mentioning the article to him, but he was touched and grateful for the number of people who went out of their way to say something positive to him. His colleagues were making it quite clear that they had no truck with what had been written about him; and Laurie went home that evening feeling that he might not, after all, be hounded out of his job.

Chapter Ten

AL

It took a while, but eventually Al managed to gather the courage to meet up with Gemma. They met in their usual place—by the clock tower in the local area of town.

They went, by mutual agreement, towards Gemma's flat. In usual circumstances, Al would have taken her hand, or put his arm around her, but he was horribly conscious of her reputation—or, rather, his lack of one. She reached out for him, but he pulled away. "I'll wait till I've got you inside," he said, smiling faintly so that she didn't take offence.

"You don't need—"

"Just go with me on this one," he asked, looking steadily at her. "I feel like I've fucked up enough people's lives. I could do without having yours on my conscience as well. Being seen with me is one thing; being seen *with* me is another."

She gave way. "Okay. But please note: I'm doing it under protest."

"Protest duly noted," he assured her. "And appreciated. I'll show you how much once I have you to myself."

She rolled her eyes, but took him home without objecting further, kissing him hard when they were through her front door.

"I presume I'm allowed to do this now?" she teased.

"Believe me," said Al, his arms full of beautiful woman, "very much so."

A while later, other appetites curbed, they sat on Gemma's luxurious sofa drinking wine and cuddling. They'd kept off the subject of *that article* until this point, but Al had known it would insist on raising its head eventually. He was resigned to it by now, and goodness knew Gemma deserved to have her say. She had continued to be supportive all through the time they hadn't been meeting in person, sending him texts about her day, or silly jokes. Just keeping in touch, one way or another—making Al feel appreciated. They'd never been much for regular text contact in the past, preferring to wait until they met in person; but perhaps the newspaper coverage had had one good effect: bringing him closer than ever to Gemma. He'd always considered her a good friend, but she had proven it beyond all shadow of a doubt of late. What he hadn't expected from her, however, was one of the first things out of her mouth on the subject.

"Why don't you try telling your side of the story?" she asked, out of nowhere.

"What do you mean?" Al asked, slightly bewildered.

"Well, look. I know a journalist. She'd talk to you. Print something accurate, too. If you just shut up shop like you've been doing, everyone's going to believe that it's true. It sucks, but it's life. Trust me, I've seen it often enough."

She probably had, too. The pop music world wasn't a kind one. The papers loved to bring you down, just as much as they loved to build you up. Possibly more. *Probably* more. Scandal was always more interesting. Gemma herself, thank goodness, had never been at the centre of malicious gossip, but she must have seen it regularly happen to people she knew. Al knew, in theory, that Gemma knew plenty of stars, but it had never really bothered him. It wasn't a part of her life that she shared with him, so he rarely thought about it. But it *did* mean that in this particular scenario, she knew what she was talking about.

"What exactly do you mean?" Al asked again, more specifically.

"Give her an interview. Get the truth out there, instead of letting all the shit have its way unchallenged."

"An interview? Seriously?" Al looked at Gemma dubiously. "Don't you think there's been publicity enough?"

She leaned forward and stroked the side of his face sympathetically. "I know what you mean, darling, but it's all one-sided at the moment. Hel's nice. She's reliable. She'd write something true. Give you a chance to put your side of things."

"I'm not up for revenge or crap like that," Al said firmly.

"You're a better man than me. I would totally be spitting nails. But no, I didn't think you would be—it's not your style, is it, darling? But if the films are suffering... And your blokes? How are they doing?"

Al pulled a face. "We've pulled things back together. Sort of. Mostly. Laurie's work can't penalise him, even if they wanted to, though in fact his workmates have been pretty supportive, on the whole. But he's been accused of nothing illegal, and they've got none of his students claiming he's made a move on them, thank fuck. God knows it would only take one person saying he had, and things would be a hundred times worse. Not that they truthfully could, since—well, you know Laurie. Seriously?"

"Yeah. I know," Gemma agreed. "It wouldn't cross his mind." She grinned. "I reckon he's got his hands more than full enough with you and James anyway. You, especially."

Al chuckled. "I've got you and various other people. It's James you want to look out for. He's a bloody sex maniac."

She laughed. "I can't believe you said that," she said in mock outrage. "I'll tell him, if you're not careful."

She would as well, Al knew. He'd rather like to see Jamie's face if she did.

"So, as far as Laurie's concerned, it's not the end of the world. Though he's very"—Al wasn't going to give away any secrets which weren't his own, but he was bothered a little by Laurie. They were still having sex, but Laurie was passive, gentle, almost reluctant in bed. Al sometimes thought he'd do anything for a bit of the old, dominating Laurie—"reserved, still, at the moment."

"Yeah," Gemma said sympathetically. "Well, it'll take time, probably."

"Still, it burns me up that she gets to write all of that about him, and I just have to sit and take it," Al admitted. "I feel like it's my fault, you know?"

Gemma leaned forward so she was forehead to forehead with him. "That's ridiculous," she said patiently. "You're not responsible for some bitch's lies."

"Yeah, but... Well, you know all that." Al sighed. "Go on then, tell me about this friend of yours."

Gemma shrugged, sitting up and taking a sip of her drink. "She's not a close friend, precisely, just a journo I've got to know and have met a few times for a coffee. You know, I see a fair few. But she covers the arts in general—music, plays, films. So she's someone who could do a piece on you and it would sit nicely in her area. And I can tell you something— she wouldn't write lies, and everyone in the business knows it. If you want a respected name to back you, Hel Gerrard's a decent option."

Now Gemma had given the whole name, it seemed familiar. She wrote for a bigger magazine than those which usually covered Al's work, but Al was interested in films in general and read around on the subject. Of course, living with a film studies lecturer made that more than easy to do: Laurie usually had a lot of material lying around.

"And you reckon she'd talk to me?" Al asked.

"I was speaking to her a few days ago, and I mentioned you and she said she'd be interested in talking with you. I said I didn't know how you'd take it, so I haven't committed you or anything," Gemma said hastily. "And if you think I've overreached myself, I'm sorry. I know it's none of my business, and—"

"Gem..." Al put his finger to her lips. "Shh. I'm pretty sure this woman wouldn't touch me with a barge pole if you didn't know me. She sounds totally out of my league." He smiled. "A bit like you. I'm grateful. Thank you."

Thus it was that a couple of days later, Al was entering a café in a suburb of London he didn't know at all. Hel had texted him a picture of herself and arranged a time and place. Al, early as usual, discovered that on this occasion the journalist was earlier still. He walked over, trying to look casual and unconcerned.

"Hi. I'm Al."

He slipped into the seat opposite Hel, giving her a small smile and an appraising look. He had spent most of the journey by tube berating himself for being idiot enough to do this. James and Laurie had both been understandably wary when he told them what he was doing, and the closer he got to meeting Hel, the more he wished he'd never come. However, it was too late now. The only thing was to be as honest as possible, and hope for the best. That in itself wouldn't be too problematic: honesty was natural to Al. But given the details of some of the things he had to talk about, he was more than aware that it was not going to be a comfortable experience.

"Hel Gerrard." Hel held out a hand. She was in her early thirties, Al guessed (and he was pretty experienced at this sort of summing up), with long, dark hair drawn back in a ponytail and was wearing a dark-red top with blue jeans. Al could see that she was assessing him in the same fashion he was her and wondered what she made of him. Time would tell. "I gather you're a friend of Gemma's?" she added.

"Yes."

Al added nothing more. He was pretty sure that anyone who knew Gemma—and had read about him—could connect the dots to know precisely what sort of friendship they had, but he had no intention of confirming it. He had never kissed and told in his life, and he had no intention of starting now.

Hel's appraisal continued. "She doesn't always have the best taste in men," she commented. "But apparently you've known each other for a while, and she usually sees through them pretty quickly."

"I'm subtle," Al retorted lightly, smiling.

Hel raised her eyebrows. "Funny; that's not the impression I've been getting, reading about you."

Al's smile faded. "Fair enough. Do you mind if I order a coffee?"

"Be my guest. I'm sorry," Hel said abruptly. "I'm not here to give you a bad time. I just...wasn't sure what to expect."

"I can't say I'm at my most comfortable with journalists just at the present moment," Al said, trying to sound friendly under severe provocation.

He went to order his coffee and brought it back to the table. It would make a barrier, if nothing else: something to hold between himself and Hel if necessary. If this was Gemma's idea of a 'nice' journalist, Al wasn't sure he'd want to meet a nasty one. Oh right, he already had. Actually, comparatively speaking, Hel was delightful.

"So," he said, "what did you want to talk about?"

"To the point. I like that." Hel leaned back. "Tell me a bit about your films. The last two have done quite well, critically, haven't they?"

Oh, now that was an unexpected change. It was Al's turn to feel surprised—and grateful. Just about everything else written about him lately had only mentioned his films in passing, as an excuse to start banging on about his personal life. Hel would get to that, no doubt; but it was nice that she was bothering to start by talking about the films. Especially when Brooke's description of those had also been so demeaning.

"Yes. I've been lucky—there's been a great team of people working with me. *Welding the Night Away* was the first of my films to get nominated for an award, which was pretty much down to the amazing performance by Fliss Springer, who was playing Helen, the main character. It was one of those experiences where you see something you've put together become so much more, just because of the way Fliss took Helen and made her into this wonderful, convincing person." Al could talk about his films all day. He had half forgotten the reason behind the interview in his enthusiasm. "Then there was the camera work—my guys worked so hard, trying all the different techniques a million times over. I've seriously never seen any group of people put so much effort into something. The nomination was really owed to them for that."

"It's about a woman with mental health problems, isn't it?" Hel looked at him. "What drove you to make a film about mental health, and have a woman as the main character?"

Al flinched a little at the second half of the question. Was she trying to suggest anything inappropriate about his having a female lead? He turned instead to the first part. "I think mental health is an important and very much misunderstood area of life," he said instead. "When one in three people will have mental health problems at some point in their lives, the amount of money that goes into funding help with it is shockingly poor. Equally, there is still this idea that people can 'snap out of it' or that there is something fundamentally 'wrong' or 'lesser' about people who have or have had mental illness. Even," he said, thinking of Brooke's article and trying not to grit his teeth, "that they're 'mad' and should be locked up. That was everything I was *not* going for. With Helen, I wanted to show a character who was someone quite special—a very strong person. You'd have to be, to cope with everything she did and produce the amazing works of art that she did."

He went on, describing the basis of the film and the character, hesitating a second before saying, "I didn't choose a female character to have a mental illness because I wanted to suggest that women are more prone to mental illness, or 'weaker' in some way. In fact, I resent greatly the idea that having mental health problems makes you weak. I don't know precisely why she was female, to be honest; she just was." He glanced up, trying not to sound defensive. "It wasn't so I could sleep with the lead actress, either, for the record."

Hel was looking more sympathetic now. "I didn't think it was," she assured him. "I'm sorry if I gave that impression."

She drew him on to talk about *Transparent*, the more recent film, which was having astounding success for its genre and budget. At least, it had been up until recently. Al's production company had informed him that of late, the levels of interest had been wavering—and everyone knew why. They'd told him that bit, too; and Al had felt the criticism deeply.

After speaking a bit about the film itself, he forced himself to face the problem head on. Swallowing, he said: "*Transparent* hasn't been doing quite so well, recently, though. I...probably ought to say something about that. It would be a great shame and a waste if any actions—or...or...claimed actions—of mine led to the films not getting the viewings they deserve. A lot of extremely talented people poured their souls into making them, and if any recent publicity has turned anyone away, I can only apologise and send my deepest regrets to the crews involved in production."

She'd hurt his lovers and she'd hurt his films. If Brooke wanted revenge, she had it in spades. Everything Al cared about most. He felt his throat closing with the painful emotions and took a long sip of coffee, trying to recover his composure.

"You're not how I expected you to be," Hel said unexpectedly.

He looked at her suspiciously. "That's a double-edged sword."

"Look," she said, and Al was perceptive enough to notice that she was avoiding his unspoken question. "Let's be blunt. I've read what's been written, and I know better than to believe a lot of what Brooke Lingarten writes—yes, we've met—but I'll admit that it's difficult to know what to think when usually there's a lot of truth in this type of allegation. So, tell me. What is the truth? After all, Gemma likes you enough to call in a favour from me, and she's not that sort of girl."

Al hadn't realised that Hel was meeting him as a favour. Gemma had made it sound as though his name had come up in conversation, and that—realising that he was someone Gemma knew—Hel had shown an interest in interviewing him. He tried not to let his shock show on his face. He'd have to do something to thank Gemma; whatever Hel wrote about him, he knew that Gemma had intended this generously. And he knew as well, if not better, than Hel did how loath his sort-of-girlfriend was to ask for favours. He lifted his chin up and faced Hel head on.

"I am in a relationship with two men," he said bluntly. "That's quite true. And I'm very much in love with them, as it happens—maybe don't write that down—they'd die of the embarrassment. I don't want you to name them, though, please. They've been through enough publicity for several lifetimes, I think. They're very private people and have been quite badly hurt by some of the things that have been written."

He realised he was frowning and tried to wipe the expression from his face. No need to make his emotions too obvious. This interview was for putting an accurate depiction of the facts across, not letting anyone—

let alone a journalist—know how much the three of them had been devastated by what had been written about them. On the surface, they seemed closer than ever, and in many ways they were, but that wasn't the whole story. There was Laurie's sudden withdrawal of part of himself, even as in other ways he was sweeter than he'd been before. There was the anxious look in James's face, which hadn't quite gone. Then there was Al himself. He hadn't told anyone, but he kept having nightmares in which Laurie left again, and James turned on Al, telling him it was all his fault and he wished they'd never been friends. It was the closest Al had come to slumping back into depression, and he hardly dared sleep at the moment for fear of what the night might bring.

"I imagine they might be," Hel said dryly. "Especially the older one."

Emotionless as he was attempting to stay, Al couldn't help himself at this. "It's a crock of— I mean, it's—"

"A crock of shit," Hel finished for him.

Al blushed. "Yeah."

"What about you, though? If you're so in love with these two guys, what about all this stuff about you sleeping around? Is that a crock of shit, too?"

She must know it wasn't. Fortunately, Al hadn't been intending to deny it anyway. He sighed. "No. No, it's not. I don't have sex with anyone without Ja— without my partners being okay with it, but I am promiscuous. Always have been. They knew that from the start—as does anyone else I sleep with. I don't pretend about anything. I wouldn't sleep with anyone who doesn't understand my situation and agree to it." He gave a somewhat rueful smile. "Though I am definitely not as...prolific...as certain articles have made me out to be. Frankly, I'm not sure it would be humanly possible, but I don't even have the urge to try. The truth is, mostly I'm happy with my boyfriends and a couple of other semi-regular partners."

Al made sure not to meet Hel's eye at this point. He was damned if he was going to make any admissions as to whom any of these other partners might be. He hesitated. He'd already mentioned something about the crap written about Laurie, but of all the things he wanted Hel to take away from this meeting, it was a real, certain knowledge that the things written—or at least implied—about his boyfriend were out and out lies. The trouble was knowing how to express it. Finally, he said cautiously, "I don't want to talk about them much because their lives are their own business, but one thing I feel I need to say is that my partners—unlike me—*are* exclusive, and that any negative allegations made about them are utterly untrue."

"That hurt you, didn't it?" Hel said, her voice unnervingly gentle. "What was written about Dr Rose."

"They practically said he was—" Al remembered that they were in a public coffee shop, and bit back the rest of the sentence hastily. Instead, he said, "He and J—my other partner, got together when my other partner was twenty-two, for the record. And I've been living with them for a little over a year." The last was as near as he got to an untruth: he had indeed been living with Laurie and James for about a year, but they had only actually been in a relationship for approximately eight months, though they had been sleeping together on occasion for several years before that. Going into all that detail made everything far too murky, however, so the three of them had agreed on this accurate, if misleading, statement. "And...um, not with the names, do you think? Please? I know it's stupid when the whole Internet has got it stamped all over it, but—"

"Yes. Sorry. You're being very honest."

Al shrugged. "I don't see much point in lying. I've never pretended to be anything other than what I am. I just hate that it's hurting other people—and the films."

"There's one very specific accusation in the Brooke article," Hel probed.

Al knew he looked guilty. "Yes."

"Yes?"

"Mm." Well, Al had at least known this was coming. "I did say something similar to that," he said honestly. "But the circumstances were...different. I was with someone, and yes, I'd been kissing her, earlier—but then she started talking about—" He cut off suddenly. If Hel were homophobic, of course, the fact that he'd already admitted to being in love with Laurie and James was going to have sealed his journalistic fate. That his unarguably vulgar comment to Brooke had come after she had compared gay sex to bestiality would not help him in that case: he would already be beyond help. If she weren't, however, maybe she might have some degree of sympathy. And Gemma would surely not have sent him to someone who hated gays, nor would she have formed a friendship with them. He hoped. "She said," he said slowly, "that sex between 'poofs' was pretty much bestiality and expected me to agree. For fairly obvious reasons, I didn't react very well. I shouldn't have said what I did, and in hindsight, I wish I never had. It was vulgar, and…and maybe…definitely…unnecessary. I was angry, and I shouldn't have said it. Immediately after I did, I left rather abruptly and haven't seen her since. Any suggestion that anything further happened between us is untrue."

Hel gave him a long look. "Was the woman in question's name 'Brooke', by any chance?" she asked.

Al started. "What?"

How the hell…?

"It's just, I've seen her write something along those lines before."

"Oh." Al pulled himself together. There was no way he was going to confirm Hel's belief, disconcerted though he was by her percipience. "Look, I'm not giving names. Not hers, not anyone's. I just wanted—needed—to explain there was a bit more to it than it sounded. I don't go round trying to offend people. And I definitely don't—do things people don't want. I was… Most people know, you know? About me? Oh god, that makes it sound even worse. I didn't realise she didn't know I was bisexual, and then I reacted badly. And I'm sorry for it." He sighed. "It hurts when people say things like that."

"Yes. I imagine it might."

Al looked at Hel sharply. Once again, her comment could be taken in a number of ways. He still wasn't sure what he thought of her, and—more worrying still in the circumstances—what she thought of him. Plus, she could see much further through a brick wall than Al was at all comfortable with. She looked back at him blandly, clearly not intending to give anything away.

"So," she said, seemingly taking mercy on him before the pause could get too awkward—that, or setting him up for further trouble—"are you working on another film?"

Al knew the question was supposed to be a kind one (at least, he hoped it was), but unfortunately, it just brought up another issue. The truth was, he *had* been working on a new script, but his production company had told him that it would have to be put on hold until the current 'situation' had worked through. Yet again, he wondered uncomfortably whether he wasn't in the position of making everything a lot worse; bringing up the whole can of worms to wriggle around in public view once more.

"I...er..." He'd at least known that the other questions were coming. This one had taken him by surprise. He pulled himself together. He'd got this far telling the truth, he'd go on. "Yes," he said at last, "I am. But there's been a slight... I mean...the project is on hold at the moment." Hel would know what he meant by that, he knew.

She did. "You mean, until the production company decide how much of a liability you are," she said bluntly.

Al winced. It didn't sound nice put like that. Nonetheless, the fact was, it was the truth. "Yes, pretty much."

"What's it about?" she asked.

"Does it matter, in the circumstances?"

All of Al's films were about things which were precious to him. It hurt to talk about it when he didn't know whether it would be made. Especially when he knew if it wasn't, he only had himself to blame. Him, and his big mouth, and the promiscuity which left him open to this sort of accusation.

"Humour me."

And, frankly, that wasn't something Al was in a position to argue with. Sitting with a journalist who could certainly pretty much break his career entirely, even if she couldn't mend it... If Hel said jump, Al was going to have to jump. If she said she wanted to know about his latest script idea, then he would be telling her everything she wanted to know about it.

"It's about a man in his twenties who gets breast cancer—a cis man, this time," he added. He saw by Hel's expression that he'd bewildered her with this last expression and cursed himself. He always forgot the number of people who knew very little about gender identity terms. "I mean," he corrected himself, "someone who was assigned their accurate gender at birth. In other words, not trans—not like Jack, in *Transparent*."

"I see."

"It touches on some of the same issues as the last two films," Al said, "to do with mental illness and gender identity. Getting an illness so very associated with women is tough on David, the main character, so it has an effect mentally and also causes him to wonder about his gender. He starts doubting things he's always taken for granted."

Hel was listening carefully. "An unusual premise," she commented. "Do you ever worry that people will start wondering about your own gender, given your films?"

Al shrugged. "That presumes it would bother me if they did," he pointed out. He gave a wry smile. "I know it sounds disingenuous in the circumstances to say that I don't care what people say about me, but unless it's hurting people I care about, or my films, I don't—not much. Though I'd rather not be painted as a sexual predator, on the whole," he acknowledged. That one had hurt for its own sake, if he was honest with himself. "Anyway, I don't think my gender would put people off my films. The sort of people who'd care about that aren't the sort of people who'd like the films anyway." He saw she was looking sharply at him. "What?" he asked, uneasily.

"Most men having their gender identity questioned wouldn't think first of the effect it might have on their films, that's all."

She looked him up and down, thoughtfully and a little critically. Al felt uncomfortable. He genuinely didn't care whether people considered him 'properly' male or not—wasn't even, really, sure whether he thought of himself that way, if truth be told—but if it was the sort of thing which mattered to Hel Gerrard, he was in trouble. There was no doubt a beautiful story which could be told—what, that he felt less than a man, and then took it out on women by raping them? It held together wonderfully as a narrative, he was sure, and would no doubt pull readers in like nothing else. The fact that it had no resemblance to the truth (or any truth that Al had ever known) didn't seem to be something that journalists worried about too much, he thought bitterly.

He pulled on his reserves of courage. "Well. Um…is there anything else you want to ask me about?"

"Is there anything else you want to say?" she asked in return.

The question shouldn't have been alarming. But somehow it was. Al could think of nothing else that he could say, not really. Passionate declarations of his innocence of sexual abuse? Hardly. Wouldn't anyone, sexual abuser or not, say the same? A plea for people not to let their feelings about his lifestyle affect how they felt about his films? How could it not, really? Al knew it would bother him to feel he was supporting someone whose morality he loathed; it would be hypocritical to ask for different values to apply to himself. Part of him wanted to bring up Laurie again, to reiterate his boyfriends' (because James had been affected as well) complete innocence of any wrongdoing, but he was frightened of looking as if he were protesting too much.

"No," he said quietly, trying not to look as tired and depressed as he suddenly felt. "I think we pretty much covered everything."

"Indeed." Hel had closed off, and Al wondered what he'd said to make her back off like that. As if in an attempt to distract him, she smiled, but Al could see that it didn't reach her eyes. "Thank you for meeting me. It's been very informative. I'll let you have a copy of the article when it comes out."

Al forced himself to smile back. What had he done? God, what had he bloody done? Could he do nothing but fuck up time and time again? As far as he could think, he'd not said anything wrong this time, not really—nothing he could pick up on and regret. He'd been honest, but James and Laurie had been right. Seeing another journalist had been the worst idea ever. Seeing a journalist who was this famous—because Hel Gerrard was well known; she was *really* well known—had been a risk he hadn't really calculated properly in advance. Sure, his films were failing under the fallout from the Brooke article...but if Hel Gerrard slated him, he'd really know what failure was. He tried to ignore the increasing sickness in his stomach.

"It was kind of you to meet me," he said, listening distantly to his voice as it said all the right things. "Please don't think any differently of Gemma because of this. I'm sure you know she'd do anyone a favour if she could. Goodbye."

Hel reached out and shook his hand again. Her handshake was warm and firm, but she didn't meet his eyes. "Goodbye, Al."

Chapter Eleven

Laurie

"So, how did it go?" Laurie asked Al when he got back from work.

James wasn't home yet; he was teaching until seven tonight. Al was sitting on the sofa, laptop open, looking through something with rapt attention.

"Huh? Oh, sorry." Al closed down the laptop and turned to Laurie. "Hi, Laur. How was your day?"

"It would've been better if I hadn't been worrying about you and the journalist," Laurie said honestly. "What was it like?"

Al pulled a face. "Um."

"Al, you're not encouraging me here." Laurie eased onto the sofa next to him and gave him a swift kiss.

"Well, on the upside, I asked her to keep your names—you and James—out of anything she wrote, and I'm pretty sure...well, I'm certain...she'll do that," Al offered.

"That's good." But it was difficult to sound too pleased when Al still sounded so bothered.

Al clearly gave himself a mental shake. "Look, it was probably fine," he said, trying to inject a positive note into his voice. "I mean, she didn't treat me like shit; she asked about the films, and I don't think I said anything too bloody stupid, for once in my life."

"Sounding good so far," Laurie said, leaning back and stretching long legs out in front of him. "What's the catch?"

Al sighed. "Just. I don't know what she thought of me, at all. Look, it's probably absolutely fine. I'm just paranoid. She did seem reasonably nice, after the beginning—apparently I wasn't what she was expecting, which could be taken in a fair few ways. Depends whether she meant 'after what had been written' or 'after what Gemma had said about me'. Gem would've overtalked me, but I'm not the person the article claimed, either, and it would be nice to think it's blazingly obvious." He took a deep breath. "On the other hand, she pointed out that most accusations of the nature of the ones made about me are usually true. In other words, if someone says you're a sexual abuser, you probably are. And she asked about the next film and…it sucks, Laurie, you know? Who knows if there's going to be another film—now, ever. I… I can't…" He dumped the laptop on the floor and put his head in his hands, pulling at unruly dark hair. "I can't hack the idea of not making another film," he admitted. "I was just looking through the script. It's so close to being done, but what the fuck's the point? What's the point in any of it?"

Laurie remembered how he'd felt, worrying that his job was at risk. He tugged Al sideways into his arms.

"It won't come to that, our Al," he said.

"No?" Al leaned back against Laurie, looking unseeingly at the ceiling. "If Hel Gerrard slates me, it will," he said bleakly. "I didn't quite… It'll take so little for the production company to dump me. And no one else will take me. It's not like I'm making populist films, is it? Mental health and transgender issues? Who the fuck cares? And the sort of people who do care are also the sort of people—rightly—who are going to avoid anything directed or written by someone who's guilty of sexual assault. You know they are."

"You're not guilty of it," Laurie pointed out, stating the obvious. "And if this woman is any sort of journalist, she's not going to run anything saying you are unless she's sure. She can't be sure, because you aren't."

"I guess. Sorry. Sorry. I've had nothing to do this afternoon but sit here and think 'what if?'" Al confessed.

"And it doesn't sound like there's any reason to think she hated you, from what you've said," Laurie continued, trying to do for Al what James had done for him. He knew, better than anyone, how difficult it was to see the wood for the trees when you were looking at the disintegration of your working life, especially when you loved it.

"Don't you hate me, Laurie?" Al asked. "For putting us through this?"

"You are in a bad way, aren't you?"

"Just thinking about losing it all— My work…" Al cut off. "No," he said, with a clear effort. "You're right. It'll be fine. And even if it isn't, there's nothing I can do about it. Apart from stop drowning myself in self-pity. Not a great look. Sorry."

"Oh, shut up." Laurie kissed the top of his boyfriend's head. "You're allowed a moment here and there. You've done wonders trying to cheer up me and James as we mope, when it's affected you as much as any of us—probably more. I should have been more supportive, and I'm sorry."

"My bloody fault," Al said, for about the millionth time.

"No, love, it isn't," Laurie corrected him. "Neither James nor I have ever said that or even thought it. You did nothing wrong. You made one vaguely ill-advised remark to... I don't have words to describe the Lingarten woman...and there is no way you could possibly imagine she'd do anything as evil as this."

"I sleep around."

"And I've got two younger boyfriends."

"Who appreciate you greatly." Al turned and wound an arm around Laurie's neck. "Thanks, Laurie. Want a glass of wine? Because I think I could do with one. Didn't want to start drinking on my own, feeling like shit. But quite frankly, I've been thinking about the bottle of Pinot Grigio in the fridge for the past two hours. And I'm working at Fen's tomorrow, so I can pick up some more if it's any good."

"Sounds great. And Al—stop worrying about the interview, okay? It's done, now. She'll write whatever she wants to write, and we'll cope. If you have to put out the films independently of anywhere, we'll help you do that. God knows someone in the department at work is sure to have contacts who can help." The door began to open, and Laurie gave Al a shove. "You get the wine. I'll have a word with James, save you going over it all again. But move your computer, or James'll stand on it. You know what he's like."

Al laughed, getting to his feet and putting his laptop prudently on the desk at the side of the room before retreating to the kitchen.

"Wine, James?" he called en route, as James pushed open the door, guitar slung over his back.

"Great. White, please."

"You didn't have an option," Al informed him.

"How did it—"

"I'll tell you," Laurie said hastily.

"Oh." James put the guitar in the corner with his others and came over to the sofa. "Bad as that?" he asked, in a low voice.

"No. At least," said Laurie warily, "I don't think so. Al's just having a fit about his career. I think she brought it home to him how much he loves making films, and how close he's come to losing it."

"Ni-ice," James commented.

"Oh, not intentionally, necessarily. He's just—well, I've not seen him like this before." Laurie was more anxious than he had wanted to show

Al. Al's negative mood was out of character. At all other points, he'd been offering solutions, ideas, or at least apologies. This clear feeling of helplessness was not at all natural.

"Hmm."

"We could try and distract him, though?" Laurie suggested.

James looked hopefully at Laurie at this, and Laurie shrank back into the sofa, knowing what James was thinking. Pushing Al into subspace would take him out of himself, but Laurie couldn't do it. He wasn't sure he'd ever be able to go there again, quite truthfully. Al wasn't the only one struggling with the after-effects of the newspaper article. He shook his head slightly.

"What we were talking about the other day," he said, instead. "You and him. You know."

James went very still, his dark eyes searching Laurie's. "Are you certain you're okay with it?" he asked.

James wanted Al to fuck him. It had been tough for Laurie to hear that, when James had told him; one of the foundations of their relationship had been the fact that James had waited years for Laurie, never bottoming for anyone else until he got together with the man he'd desired for so long. When James had said that he wanted another partner in a way he'd only previously wanted Laurie…it had been painful, even though that partner was Al. But Laurie knew that was selfish of him. And he couldn't deny James anything, especially something which he was pretty certain Al had always been interested in doing. Al would never have said anything, of course: Al wasn't like that. He'd always bent over backwards to avoid doing anything that might damage Laurie and James's relationship, or even tread on their toes in the slightest. But if it was something James wanted too… Laurie would have to have been a harder man than he was to refuse them. And with Al being in such a state, the last of Laurie's reservations had melted away. If anything could take Al out of the funk in which he had been when Laurie got home, it was this.

"I'm okay with it," he said, kissing James. "I just suggested it, remember."

James put his hands to Laurie's face, holding him and looking into his eyes. "It makes no difference to us. You know that, don't you?"

But it did, of course. Laurie suspected they both knew it. And he couldn't lie.

"I want you to have everything you want. And Al to have everything he wants," he said instead. "I couldn't ever be happy, knowing you could be happier. I'm okay with it, Jamie. Trust me." He gave a quick smile. "I'm trusting you."

"Love you," James whispered against his neck, pulling him close. "You have no idea."

"Love you too."

Laurie wrapped his arms around James, holding him tight. Fighting back the slightly choky feeling inside himself. He couldn't—didn't—doubt James's love for him, no matter how undeserving of it he sometimes felt.

Al reappeared, holding three glasses of wine. "Anyone for— Sorry, interrupting something?"

"Nothing which wouldn't be better for your involvement," Laurie said, turning to smile at him. "Why don't we take the wine into the bedroom?"

Al raised his eyebrows. "Sounds promising. Hey, Jamie—are you going to talk to me today, or what?"

"Nope," said James. He let go of Laurie gently and went to give his other boyfriend a careful hug around the wine before taking one of the glasses from him. "I'm bored of you. Nearly sixteen years of friendship and that's quite enough. Plus, I asked about your day earlier, and you haven't asked about mine. Clearly I'm not important to you."

"I offered you wine," Al protested.

Laurie rolled his eyes. James and Al's ability to interact as if they were still teenagers was both entertaining and frustrating at once. James caught his reaction and gave him a big grin.

"Wine, Laurie?"

Laurie took James's wine from him and went into the bedroom with it, leaving James to give an objecting yelp. He heard Al give a soft laugh, and the childish gesture was worth it for that alone. Laurie placed his wine glass on the bedside table and propped himself up against the headboard. James clambered on next to him, slinging an arm around Laurie. Laurie spread his legs a little way apart and pulled Al between them, careful of the two glasses Al still held. He sat with James like this regularly; less often with Al. It felt different—Al was so much smaller that his head half rested against Laurie's shoulder when he leaned back. Al took a gulp out of one of the wine glasses before placing them both next to Laurie's. He then wriggled comfortably into position, a movement which had a predictable effect on Laurie's libido.

"Don't think I don't know you're doing that on purpose," Laurie said scoldingly.

"Mm." Al leaned his head right back on Laurie's shoulder and gave him a little smile. "Feels good."

He leaned over and took another long sip of his wine. Laurie did the same, running his other hand under Al's shirt in an almost absent-minded fashion as he did so.

"You're doing that on purpose, too," Al said, relaxing into Laurie's touch.

"You don't say," Laurie said dryly.

"Anyone going to let me join in?" James asked teasingly.

Laurie turned his head and took James's mouth in a leisurely kiss. "We could consider it," he assured him.

Al ran a hand down James's leg. "You going to make it worth my while?"

James and Laurie exchanged a look: Laurie's glance full of amusement, James's with a little trepidation. His boyfriend was nervous about this, Laurie realised.

"Maybe," James drawled.

"Tease," Al threw back; but his hand took up a position on James's thigh, stroking in a sensual, repetitive motion.

The gestures got steadily more intimate as the wine disappeared, the clothes vanishing in almost direct proportion to the alcohol until there was barely anything of either left. James straddled Laurie, kissing him hard and passionately. Laurie knew that James was trying to show him how much he cared; to prove that what they'd agreed for the evening made no difference to how James felt about him. He ran one hand down James's back, pulling him close, whilst he tangled his other through Al's hair.

"God, you two have no idea how fucking great you are together," Al said, his voice deep with sex.

"Not so bad yourself," James muttered between kisses.

Laurie allowed himself to revel in the sensation of James pressed hard up against him, committing to memory the muscle and bone of his back, the way James's light evening stubble felt against his face.

"Everything you want," he whispered in James's ear, giving it a gentle nibble whilst he was there.

James leaned back and smiled at him, that heart-stopping smile which would make a stronger man than Laurie do anything to receive it.

"I think Al wants a go," James said.

James slid off Laurie's lap, reaching for his glass, in which resided the last of the wine. Al was lying down, and he pulled Laurie down next to him. Laurie went willingly, placing long, slow kisses down the side of Al's neck before turning his attention to his mouth. Al had been stroking himself as James and Laurie kissed, and after one passionate exchange, Laurie pulled back to admire the beautiful lithe figure which was Al. He was not so small as to reasonably be called fragile, but he was slender and toned, his pale skin making the red of his aroused and erect cock stand out in contrast.

"God, you're hot," Laurie said, slipping a hand over Al's chest and down to his abdomen, where he rested it gently, just centimetres from Al's erection.

"And you're a tease," Al retorted with a smile, wriggling so that he was lying half across Laurie, one of his legs sliding between Laurie's larger two.

"Mm-hm," Laurie acknowledged, wrapping his arms over Al's torso and pulling him more firmly on top of him.

James had finished the wine and lain down beside the pair of them, propped on one elbow to look at them. "God, I'm so hard for you," he remarked, pushing up against their sides and rutting lightly against them.

"Well, given that," Al said, lying lazily with Laurie's arms folded around him, one foot playing gently with James's calf, "how do you two want me?"

James's eyes met Laurie's, and Laurie gave him a faint smile. There were reasons to want this, he reminded himself. So many reasons. The boys would be beautiful this way, just as they always were. Had Al said that James and Laurie were great together? James and Al took Laurie's breath away. Well, they had considerably more noticeable physical effects on Laurie than merely that, if truth be told. Watching James fuck Al was a turn-on Laurie would never get enough of. Perhaps watching things the other way around might be just as good.

And James could have left Laurie for Al a million times before. Hell, he could have chosen never to start up with Laurie; James and Al's physical relationship preceded the one between Laurie and James, thanks to Laurie's shame and fear surrounding the two of them. Yet James had always, always turned back to Laurie. Even when Laurie had run away, James had waited and welcomed him back with open arms, an open heart. Whenever Laurie had wanted him, James had been there. He could trust James beyond all limits, and James deserved just that.

As to Al... Alistair Richard Hitchins, once the bane of Laurie's life—in so much as a twelve-year-old kid could be a bane—and now...so very much more. Al, whom Laurie had misjudged and underestimated a thousand times; who had known about James's feelings for Laurie and supported his best friend, no matter what; who had taken the blame for a situation far beyond his control or fault; who had offered to leave everything he knew and loved, just to keep both James and Laurie happy... How could Laurie refuse Al anything, even something the young man didn't know he might be offered?

"James?" Laurie prompted.

The love in James's face would have made anything worth it. There was a long, long look between the two of them before Laurie's boyfriend—his original boyfriend—turned to Al.

"Al," said James, softly, "fuck me."

Laurie felt Al stiffen in his arms. He kissed Al's neck reassuringly, trying to tell him silently that it was okay.

"What?" said Al, after a blank pause of a few seconds.

James leaned forward and kissed Al long and gently on the mouth. "I asked you once before," he said, "but this is different, I think? Will you?"

"Laurie..." Al started, dubiously.

"Is right here and hasn't objected," Laurie said, stroking his hands over Al, and craning his neck to kiss James across Al's body.

"I... Jesus, James, are you sure?"

It took a lot to put that level of shock into Al's voice, but James had managed. Behind the shock, however, Laurie could hear a desperate desire, a feverish hope. It had been hard for Laurie to give James the unwavering encouragement to go ahead with this. But he had, and listening to that wistful, needy note as Al spoke, Laurie knew it was right. James wanted this. Al *more* than wanted this. He was almost pleading with James to allow him to do it. It still hurt, a bit, that Laurie wasn't enough for James, even though he knew that James didn't see it like that. But Laurie would give his lovers anything and everything he could—and this was the gift they wanted.

"Why? Not keen?" asked James, jokingly but with a little undercurrent of uncertainty. Apparently, he could not hear the same things in Al's voice that Laurie could.

"Not... Bloody hell, Jamie." Al reached out his hands and began to touch James all over, as if making certain he was really there, and this wasn't just a figment of Al's fevered imagination. "Very keen," he confessed, his green eyes taking in James greedily. "But only if you're sure, Jamie. It's not something you can take back. You need to be sure you won't regret it in the morning."

Laurie clenched his fists in a flash of anger. And this was the man that Brooke Lingarten had as near as anything accused of sexual assault. This young man, the one who was holding back from what he wanted to do more than anything else, just to be absolutely certain that it was what his partner wanted too.

James gave a little huff of amusement. "Depends how bad you are at it," he teased, grinning mischievously at his best friend.

Al laughed out loud at that, and Laurie grinned. His boyfriends would never grow up, and it turned out he liked them like that.

"Bastard," Al said, changing the style of his touching and tickling James until he squealed and pushed at Al's hands. "I've not had any complaints yet, thank you very much."

"Then I'm very sure," James said, leaning in to kiss Al again.

"And Laurie?"

"It's not my body," Laurie said, smiling, trying to look relaxed. "I'm going to lie here and watch you fuck James, Al, and it's going to be bloody hot because you two always are." That much at least was true.

"Bloody hell, I can't believe—" Al cut off. He moved over to James, lying on top of him and running his hands through James's hair before pressing his lips against James's. "Fuck, Jamie," he murmured, rubbing up against him. He sounded awed.

"That was the general idea, certainly," James agreed, moving his own hands over Al's back and down to his arse, and pulling him tightly in towards him.

They frotted up against each other, and Laurie watched their kisses get more and more passionate. When Al pulled his head up, he looked a bit dazed.

"Lube," he said, fumbling for the drawer. "James, you're sure?"

"Stop asking that," James scolded. "Don't I feel sure?"

He bucked up under Al, and Al made a sudden appreciative noise in his throat at the feel of James's rock-hard erection pushing against his own. "You feel sure," he admitted. He flipped the top from the lube and spread some onto his fingers. "Spread your legs for me, James," he urged, pulling back off his lover to allow him room to do so.

James repositioned himself, pressing the small of his back to the bed and pulling his knees up and out from his body, giving Al access to the most private part of him. Al put a hand between his legs, running a wet fingertip around James's puckered entrance.

"Feels good," James said, his eyes closing as he took in the sensation.

"I'm shaking," Al said, half-laughing. "God, Jamie, you make me nervous as a virgin."

"Idiot." James smiled, thinking it was a joke.

But Laurie could see that Al was speaking nothing but the literal truth. His hand trembled as he touched James so intimately. It seemed peculiar that someone who had done so many things with James in the past—been touched, and touched in so many ways—should be left so bowled over just by this. Something he must have done with a multitude of men, for goodness sake. It was hardly like Al was inexperienced. But they, Laurie reminded himself, had not been James. This was something Al had never thought he would do with James, and it clearly mattered to him. Al slid a finger inside James. This much he'd done before, though rarely. He moved it back and forth tentatively, stroking the inside of his lover, pushing in deeply and then crooking the digit round so that it rubbed gently against James's prostate. However, whilst James wasn't as needy as Al himself could be when it came to being filled, on this occasion he pushed back impatiently onto Al's finger.

"Not your fingers I was exactly after," he grumbled.

Al hitched a smile. "Well, I guess if you're used to Laurie, it's not like I'm going to break you," he acknowledged. He lubed his cock, and Laurie could tell that he was biting back the urge to ask James one more time if he was certain. "Fuck, I want you," he said instead.

"Fuck me, Al," James urged him again, and Al needed no more encouragement.

He leaned over and kissed James firmly and long before positioning himself and pushing gently against James's entrance. James reached out and took Laurie's hand in his, his eyes still on Al as he did so.

"God, you're so..." Al cut off with a groan as he pushed further inside James. James made a little noise of encouragement, arching his back and holding Laurie's hand even tighter than before. "So gorgeous, fuck," Al went on, the words quiet and desperate. "God, Jamie, fuck, can't believe I'm fucking you... God, I love you, you're so good, please..."

Al had always been a vocal lover, both in words and noises. Laurie wondered if his boyfriend realised how much his language had changed, however, over the past year. The softened words, the declarations of love. Those last were something Laurie had never imagined he'd hear from Al. He suspected Al himself did not even know what he was saying—caught up in the moment, words would tremble and fall from his mouth without his conscious will.

Al had buried himself entirely within James now and was looking down at his lover. "Tell me it's okay," he begged James.

"Please, Al," James said simply, rocking up underneath the other man.

"Fuck, yes. Wrap your legs round me, Jamie," Al said, still gazing at James with that intent expression, as if he were learning his best friend anew.

James did so, changing the angle so that his hips were barely touching the bed. Gently, Laurie disentangled his hand from James's and moved to push a pillow underneath the space; as he did so, Al turned to look at him. The expression on his face was of naked gratitude and love: even if James didn't know, Al understood that this must have cost Laurie something.

"Oh, Laur," he breathed, the words so quiet that if Laurie hadn't been so focused, he might not have heard them.

Laurie smiled back at him and murmured, "Beautiful," making Al blush and duck his head.

James turned his head a little, noticing the byplay, and smiled at Laurie, running his fingertip across Laurie's lips before turning back to Al.

"Touch yourself. Bring yourself off for me," Al urged James, making the smallest of movements inside him, just millimetres in and out. "I want to watch you."

"Tease," James murmured, before bringing his hand round to his cock and sliding a loose fist up and down his shaft. Laurie, unable to help himself, wrapped his fingers round James's own, and together they wanked him. James made a small noise of pleasure at the gesture before looking up at Al. "Fuck me harder."

There was a small smile on Al's face at this request, and he began to move in and out of James with more purpose. "Thought you'd never ask," he said.

Laurie's other hand was on his own prick because his boyfriends were beautiful like this. Al always gave all of himself in sex. It was new and strange to see him in this more dominant role, but there was something quintessentially Al-like about the way he made love to James, something curiously familiar even as it was so different. Laurie stroked himself lazily, watching Al thrust into James's arse with long, hard movements. The change of position meant that James's prostate was under constant pressure every time Al drove into him. And James was making encouraging noises as their hands worked fast on his cock. Al himself was babbling words again, over and over—*fuck*, and *yes*, and *Jamie*, and *please*—moving harder still as he saw from the expression on James's face that he was getting close. Laurie, unable to help himself, moved his hand from his cock to touch James's chest, wanting to feel him come, knowing from wonderful years of experience the little jerk which his lover would give as he orgasmed. Al saw the movement and glanced at Laurie once more.

"Fucking gorgeous," he panted, looking back at James, who was moaning now, just about to come.

And Al was right. James was absolutely fucking gorgeous like this, just on the edge, sweaty and messy and hot, and Laurie loved him so damn much. He felt James jolt and looked down to watch the white, warm ejaculate pulse from James's cock as his boyfriend gasped for breath, his heart thumping against Laurie's palm. And Al was watching too, mumbling, "Jamie, Jamie," in a voice so full of love that it was hard to recognise as Al's own, before thrusting hard and dissolving into his own orgasm with an incoherent cry.

God, Laurie's boyfriends were amazing. Laurie looked at the pair of them, panting and coming, and instead of feeling the pain that he'd expected, watching someone else fuck his lover, instead, he just felt an overwhelming love and tenderness for them both. Al seemed so casual, flirting and shagging his way round half of London; yet he could look at James with that expression in his eyes, speak with that note in his voice. Laurie was pretty certain that no one else Al slept with got that particular version of his boyfriend—except perhaps Laurie himself? Certainly when Al was submitting to Laurie, Laurie knew that he was being offered a part of Al which no one else had seen. He remembered the first time they'd tried it: Al, afterwards, admitting that he hadn't realised the experience could be so intense. The wondering disbelief in Al's voice as he'd said "That was...incredible." Yet somehow, since seeing that article, Laurie couldn't bring himself to push Al into submissive mode. No matter how much he had been reassured that Al wanted it, it felt inappropriate. He could see the words in the paper again: *He has known the men intimately since they were ten years old and he more than twice their age.* Ordering around, controlling, a much younger man seemed...wrong, in a way it had not before. But if he could not do that for Al, at least James and Al had got this new experience. And Laurie knew that they had both needed his blessing. That, at least, he could give. For the first time, too, he wondered whether he might not be able to give more—some day. Al trusted him, after all; was it actually betraying his trust to shy away as Laurie was doing?

"Laurie?" James said, quietly.

Laurie put aside his concerns and turned to smile at James, who was thinking of him so soon after coming. "I knew you'd be hot together."

"You okay?" Al asked, flushed and sticky.

"After watching that? Definitely."

Al looked half-shy, as he gave a small smile, wiping his face with a slightly tremulous hand. "You'll have to do more than watch next time," he said. Then he turned uncertainly to James. "If there is a next time, obviously," he added quickly. "There doesn't need to be."

"There really does," James said, kissing him. "As long as Laurie...?"

"Does Laurie look like he minds?" Laurie asked, pulling them both towards him, sweaty and come-soaked as they were. "And I think I maybe did a little more than merely watch, you know."

"Mmm." James made a pleased sound and wriggled closer to Laurie.

Then both young men were trying to kiss him at the same moment, and there was a laughing duel for possession of Laurie's mouth before Al gave in.

"I've got my way enough this evening. I'll cede to you, Jamie," he said, nibbling his way around Laurie's ear instead.

"You have?" James asked, when he was done kissing Laurie. "I thought that was me."

"Definitely me," Al assured him, now spread out on top of Laurie, with James curled up next to them, warm against Laurie's side. "Fuck. I can't believe I just did that."

"Did *me*, you mean," James teased.

"Yeah." There was a ridiculous grin on Al's face, as if he had won the lottery.

"Glad I'm so good."

"I knew you would be," Al assured him. "I've seen Laurie shagging you enough times. Fuck. I'm going to shut up now before I say something really embarrassing."

"There's a first time for everything," James retorted. He kissed Al, and then Laurie again for good measure. "Seriously, though. Thanks. I wasn't sure…"

"Then you're an idiot."

"I told him he could be pretty sure," Laurie said lazily. "I've seen you eyeing up my boyfriend's arse, Al Hitchins."

Al still couldn't stop grinning. "Well, can you blame me?" he demanded.

Laurie laughed. "No."

"When you've finished discussing my arse, gorgeous though I'm sure it is…" James began, managing to look both embarrassed and amused simultaneously.

"Mm?" prompted Laurie.

"You've not got off yet," James pointed out.

"He hasn't?" Al looked shocked. "Blimey, I really will have to start doubting my technique." He still sounded most incredibly smug nonetheless.

James snorted. "What, you're so good people should get off just watching you?"

"Hell yeah," Al assured him, eyes glinting.

Laurie, who knew his boyfriends of old, said hastily, "No fighting over me, thank you."

"What about fighting over who gets to get you off?" Al asked, mischievously.

Laurie rolled his eyes. "Oh, bloody hell, no fighting at all, okay? And I don't need to get off every time, thank you both very much. I had an extremely enjoyable time watching you two. And believe me, Al, you do not need to doubt yourself. If James fancied making some dinner at some point, I'd be hugely appreciative, however." It was his turn to grin. "I won't ask Al—I don't really fancy a pot noodle tonight."

"I'm feeling too good even to be insulted by that end bit," Al commented.

"No," corrected James. "You know it's accurate."

"We-ell, that too," he admitted.

James stretched leisurely. "I might have a shower first, if no one minds. But there's some steak that someone bought. I expect I can find something to do with that."

"A way to a man's heart," Al murmured. "Jamie, I knew there must be some reason I loved you."

"And Laurie?" James asked.

"Ah, he's just good in bed. Plus, he washes up." Al rolled off Laurie and onto his back, putting his hands behind his head and staring up at the ceiling with a blissful expression on his face. "Fuck, but this is a good day, after all," he said.

Laurie, looking at him and remembering the vision he'd seen when he first entered the house, smiled.

Chapter Twelve

JAMES

Fortunately, they hadn't long to wait until Hel Gerrard's article came out. It was only a week later when Al received a large envelope through the post. Slitting it open, his face changed.

"Oh."

"What?" James asked.

He'd looked with interest at the letter when he got home from work, wondering who had been writing to Al in such depth. It had been hand addressed, which was unusual and meant that it almost certainly wasn't a script, or anything film-related. But he'd had time to forget about it before Al returned, so James's curiosity was piqued anew.

"It's from the journalist. Hel Gerrard." Al grimaced. "I guess at least she's been kind enough to give me prior warning of what she's going to say. From the accompanying note, it seems the article itself will be coming out tomorrow in print. This is just a copy. 'For my information', she says."

"I see," James said cautiously. "Well, you'd better read it then."

Al flashed him a slightly exasperated look. "Yes, Jamie, I'd got that far myself. I better had." He squeezed his eyes shut for a second. "Wish me luck?"

James sighed. How was it fair that Al's career boiled down to whether he could convince one journalist that he was a decent person? How was it fair, come to that, that his life—their lives—had almost been ruined by one vindictive woman?

"Yeah," he said softly. "You know I do."

"Thanks."

Hel Gerrard's article was long. James watched Al read it with anxious interest, looking at the way his boyfriend's face tinged pink. Al had a very expressive face, and for someone with the lifestyle he led was amusingly susceptible to blushing. The question was: was he flushing with anger or embarrassment...and why?

"What's she say?" James asked when he couldn't bear it any longer. Surely Al had had time to read it all through by now? He didn't read *that* slowly, even if the article had been lengthy.

Al passed it across, and James began to scan his eyes down it, certain lines and phrases jumping out and catching his eye. Like the following, early on:

Al Hitchins is a surprisingly quiet young man, though undeniably attractive. After the newspaper allegations, I had somehow expected someone more ebullient; larger than life. Instead, I am met by a slender, dark-haired man, who greets me with the softly spoken words, "Hi. I'm Al."

Well, that was a good start. She didn't sound like she was going to slate him. James read on. There was a long and very interesting description of Al's films, couched in positive terms. James, reading it, tried to remember what had been in the Brooke article about the films. That part of it had never really drawn his attention in the circumstances, though he had a vague feeling that she had managed to take a swipe at those in passing as well. But Hel Gerrard, from what both Al and Laurie had said, was a considerably more respected authority. She wasn't quite saying that Al was a genius, but she was clearly impressed with his talent.

James felt a knot untangle in his heart. Al deserved this. God, how he deserved it. He was bloody talented. Of course, Hel might be about to go on and say that for all that, the man himself was a reprobate who deserved the worst censure, but somehow it didn't read as if she was going to. Ah. Here it came.

It is he who first introduces the difficult topics, in fact, saying quietly, "It would be a great shame and a waste if any actions—or claimed actions—of mine led to the films not getting the viewings they deserve. A lot of extremely talented people poured their souls into making them, and if recent negative publicity has turned anyone away, I can only apologise and send my deepest regrets to the crews involved in production."

I take the opportunity he has given me, and mention that there has been a lot of things written, both in newspapers and online, about his private life. What is the truth of it, I ask. He acknowledges that he is in a loving, long-term relationship with two men, but asks that their names are kept out of this article. "They're very private people and have been quite badly hurt by some of the things that have been written."

So, given that he is evidently smitten by his boyfriends...

James looked up and raised an eyebrow. "Smitten?"

"Fuck off." Al's blush seeped down his neck at this.

James grinned. Al was fun to tease. And it was definitely looking hopeful, in terms of the article. It still felt weird, seeing himself referred to in a newspaper article, even without his name attached, but he could live with this sort of comment. If he were honest (and used that sort of language), he was 'smitten' with his Al, too. Life without Al would be like living without half of himself. He couldn't imagine it—and when he tried, he gave a brief shudder. James had always been so in love with Laurie that his feelings for Al had somehow...never been quite so obvious. He suddenly realised that his feelings for his best friend and other love were just as deep, just as strong, albeit different. Holding the article in one hand, he pulled Al to him and kissed him hard. Al responded willingly, just as he always did.

"What was that for?" Al asked, when James let him go. "Not that I'm complaining, obviously. Just..." He trailed off.

"Because I love you, you daft bugger," James said. He kissed him again, more gently. "Quite a lot, actually," he added. "Anyway, stop distracting me. I'm trying to read this article."

"I'm distracting *you*?" Al demanded, but he looked pleased, nonetheless.

James returned to reading.

So, given that he is evidently smitten by his boyfriends, would it be fair to say that the allegations that he sleeps around are untrue? He meets my gaze openly. "No," he says, clearly. "I would not have sex with anyone without my partners' consent, but I am promiscuous. But I don't," he adds firmly, "sleep with anyone who doesn't understand my situation and agree to it." He gives a swift smile. "Though I am definitely not as...prolific...as certain articles have made me out to be." He hesitates a second, leaving me to wonder what he's missing out. Then he speaks again, carefully. "I don't want to talk about them much because their lives are their own business, but one thing I feel I need to say is that my partners—unlike me—are exclusive, and that any negative allegations made about them are utterly untrue." He is trying to conceal it, but I think this is the one thing which has angered him above all in the recent furore: that those he loves have been dragged through the mud alongside him.

James thought back to the first article. Handing it to Al. The first comment Al had made had been: "Laurie's going to kill me." It had never been about Al himself. His thoughts had been for the other two from the very beginning. That first night, he'd been too busy looking after James himself to throw a fit about what had happened to his own life, given the so-called revelations in the paper. James took a moment to feel rather ashamed about that. He should have been looking after Al, not vice versa. The paper had barely mentioned James; he had nothing in particular to worry about—apart from being outed at work, that was, but thankfully there had been little fallout from that. They'd already known he was gay, of course; Laurie had been around to the shop too many times for that to be in doubt. But being outed as polyamorous was actually far more scandalous in this day and age than the gay thing. (James took a moment to consider the fact that he had actually thought the phrase 'the gay thing'. In his school days—which were not all *that* far behind him, thank you very much—being gay would have been considered much more than 'a thing'. There was a reason he'd not come out until he'd left.) Having two blokes in his life, however...that had been the real shock to his workmates, the situation which made them look at him askance.

None of James's students, thank god, knew that the James Cape caught up in the Hitchins scandal was the same person as James-the-music-teacher. He didn't think many of them had known his surname in the first place, and it was hardly a rare one, after all. Plus, he had been described in Brooke Lingarten's article as a 'shop worker', so anyone who knew him as a guitar teacher would hardly be likely to associate him with the man described. And James's work colleagues had, to his intense relief, been low-key in their reaction. He'd felt a few of them giving him astonished, appraising looks, as if trying to reconcile this new information with what they already knew—or thought they knew—about James, who was, he suspected, generally thought to be relatively straight-laced, given his preference for staying in rather than partying, even in his immediate post-university days. They'd all met Laurie before, of course. But a slightly older boyfriend who worked at the local uni was hardly going to leave James with a scandalous reputation: anything but, in fact. So James could hardly be surprised that there was a certain level of interest in this new take on his previously seemingly mundane life. There had also been a ribald comment or two, which

James wasn't sure whether he was supposed to have overheard or not and had let wash over him without reply. Still, he'd gone through worse in his last year of school, standing shoulder to shoulder with an out-and-proud bisexual Al in a school where 'gay' was the generalised insult of choice, and actually to be called a 'fag' was the greatest abuse of all. The other students hadn't known about James's own sexuality—though his friendship with Al had brought innuendos from certain of the pupils, which James had refused to dignify with a response—but that had almost made defending Al even more of a duty. Something he wasn't doing for his own reputation but in defence of Al. *Plus ça change, plus c'est la même chose.* Except, on this occasion, his own reputation really had been on the line, James supposed.

James skimmed through a bit more, coming to another meaty comment from Hel Gerrard, this time on the 'violation' claim Brooke had made.

When I ask him about the specific allegation in the original article about an unpleasant explicit comment he made to a woman he was kissing, which she says made her feel violated, he looks uncomfortable for the first time. Nonetheless, his honesty remains. "I did say something similar to that," he admits, "though in circumstances rather different to those described. The woman in question—" He refuses point blank to name her. "—had just drawn a comparison between homosexuality and bestiality which I found extremely offensive. In hindsight, I should not have replied as I did, however." It was, he acknowledges, undeniably vulgar—though if his description of the conversation is accurate, perhaps somewhat understandable. The implication that anything worse might have happened appears to have no basis in truth; he says that his reaction after speaking was to leave precipitately.

I am impressed most of all by his honesty. He is clearly no fool, so must have known that this would not be the easiest of interviews. But he has come prepared to answer questions, and he does so unflinchingly, refusing to shirk even those responses which he must know may cause controversy. I find myself liking him more and more.

"She says she liked you," James commented.

"Yeah. Could've fooled me," Al said. Then, ruefully, "Mind you, I wasn't in a position to be judging anything particularly well just then."

"Apart, apparently, from what you said to her," James pointed out.

"Luck of the draw, mate." Al gave a sudden grin. "Well, that and my natural charm, obviously. Did you notice the 'undeniably attractive' bit early on?"

"Fuck off, Hitchins. You're such an egotist," James said, smiling.

"You love me for it."

James raised two fingers, fighting the urge to laugh. There was a little more about Al's personal life, and it made interesting reading. Hel Gerrard had clearly done some investigating, not just trusting her own instinctive liking for Al. James could see why she was considered a good journalist.

After meeting him, I decided to do a bit of research of my own. Unlike Brooke, I found it easy to persuade women—and men—to speak about their experiences with Al Hitchins, and the comments were invariably positive. He was described variously as "a caring and generous lover", "a great deal of fun", and "a genuinely nice person", whilst one woman added that the sex she had shared with him made up "one of the best nights I've had". Al himself, incidentally, declined to name any of his lovers, saying that such things should remain private.

However, I think the most telling point comes from a couple of people—one male, one female—who had strikingly similar stories to tell. They spoke of going on a date with Al, during which time a great deal of alcohol was drunk. Al, they say, did indeed take them back to their houses, but far from taking advantage—both respondents admit freely that they encouraged him to do so—he saw them safely home and then left them on the doorstep with a kiss. "He told me I was a very beautiful woman," said the lady, "and that he hoped to see me again when I was in a position to consent to sex." The gentleman described an occasion in almost identical terms.

James felt another rush of love for Al, reading this. He knew that Al refused to sleep with anyone if he thought they were too drunk to give proper consent. Well, he knew from personal experience that taking advantage of someone in a vulnerable situation was the last thing on earth that Al would do, in fact. But there was something rather touching about seeing it written down. And that he would leave his non-conquests in such a kind fashion, leaving them feeling positive about the situation and themselves—positive enough that two of them had come forward to tell this story, in fact, which was telling in itself—was... Well, it was very Al. A strange lad, his best friend/boyfriend. But rather a special one. No, James corrected himself: a very special one.

The article ended with a description of the next film that Al was planning, with strongly worded enthusiasm for it. Hel touched gently on the fact that it was currently 'being considered' by the production company—more tactful than the truth: that it had been ditched, possibly permanently, following the scandal—and made it clear that she hoped it would go ahead. She added, as if by chance, that she suspected that better viewing figures for *Transparent* would probably encourage the company.

"Well," exclaimed James, looking up at the end of this screed, "Fuck me!"

Al grinned. There was a light back in his eyes which had been missing since the day he'd visited Hel Gerrard. Heck, probably longer than that: since the day the Brooke article had come out.

"Any time you want," he said willingly.

James rolled his eyes. "You know what I meant. Though you probably don't need to fuck anyone right now. After all, she practically sucked you off in print, here, didn't she? And there you were wondering whether she was going to ruin you."

Al looked at him hopefully. "It's good, isn't it?" he asked, surprisingly needing reassurance in the circumstances.

James dropped the article on the table and put his arms around Al instead. "Good? Anyone reading this would think you're sleeping with her, for god's sake." He eyed his boyfriend thoughtfully. "You're not, I take it?"

Al raised his hands to James's shoulders and gave him a bit of a shove. Not enough to be likely to dislodge his grip of Al's waist, James noticed, but enough to make a point. "Fuck off. You know I'm not. Anyway, she had a wedding ring." He raised an eyebrow. "I notice these things."

"Mm." James kissed the side of Al's head, running his hands over Al's arse and thinking how right Hel was. Al was, indeed, attractive. Also, Al was *his*. He was James's and Laurie's, in a way he was no one else's, no matter how many other people he slept with. James didn't give a toss about that, quite frankly. When it came to what—to who—mattered, James was pretty confident of where he stood. He felt his lips curving in a smile.

"What?"

"Thinking about your arse," James said truthfully.

Al gave a snort at this. "What, I give you an article to read which might affect my entire future, but you're hung up on my bum?"

James's smile grew. "Pretty much, yeah. Put it this way, I don't think you need to worry too much about your career. Isn't Hel Gerrard about...ooh, ten times better read and more important than Brooke Lingarten?"

"A hundred," Al said. "Of course, scandal sells better than something saying what a decent bloke I am, but—"

"You're still a decent bloke with a thoroughly indecent private life, albeit totally consensual," James pointed out. "Even in that article. And talking of indecent..."

"You're still on about my arse," Al said, trying to sound indignant, and failing dismally.

James couldn't remember the last time he felt this happy. He couldn't remember the last time Al had looked this happy. Fuck, but life was good like this.

"Complaining?"

"Yes."

"Liar."

Al tilted his head to one side. "Yes," he admitted.

James put his mouth to Al's and kissed him, starting slowly. He licked at Al's lips, then opened his mouth just the tiniest bit against his boyfriend's, only progressing further when Al started to respond. And Al was always so responsive, once he began. He pressed his entire body closer to James, moulding into him as if he was meant to fit there, sighing softly as he reached up to hold James's head with one hand. James kissed him more passionately then, mouth opened wide, almost devouring Al. Demanding more, which Al gave willingly. Al started to roll his hips against James, and James was almost undone. He dragged Al to the sofa, pulling the smaller man down against him onto it.

"God, yes, Jamie," Al said, tearing his mouth away from James just for long enough to say the words before returning to kissing him.

Al was lying on top of James, just as James loved it. He tangled his fingers through James's, pushing their hands up on either side of James's head and grinding his hips down so that his erection pushed and throbbed against James's own. Then he dropped his head forward so that his mouth was against James's neck. James could feel Al sucking, and knew he would have a mark there tomorrow. He didn't care.

Whatever Al was doing, it felt bloody good and he wanted him to keep on. For a while Al did, but then he pulled away with a groan.

"Fuck, Jamie, how can you make me feel so much like I'm a teenager again and could come just from doing this?" he demanded, leaning down and kissing James again, deliberately lightly.

"Don't stop," James pleaded.

Al was breathing hard. "Got to. Told you, going to come just like this, fully bloody clothed, if I don't. See what you do to me, Jamie." He closed his eyes for a few seconds, as if grounding himself. "Fuck. Want you so much."

"Then fucking take me," James said, hot and frustrated.

"Trying to think. Give me a sec. When's Laurie due back?"

"Soon. I hope."

James sighed, and manoeuvred so that he was sitting up, Al still half lying on him, one leg thrown firmly across his crotch. James shifted a bit, desperate for pressure against his cock, loving the way Al's jeans-clad thigh was shoved against his own lighter materialed trousers and rubbed hard against his erection. He wanted to frot up against Al, feeling the friction over and over again, but with an intense determination, he forced himself to stay still.

"Just wondered if we should wait for him," Al said. "God, you scramble my brain when you do things like that. I was about ten seconds away. Do you know that?"

"And then you stopped. Bloody tease," James grumbled.

"What, you don't want Laurie?" Al smiled wickedly. "Gone off him, have you?"

That was deliberate provocation, and James pushed Al off him at his words. Al, not expecting it, made a wild grab at nothing and slid gracelessly onto the floor in a tangle of arms and legs.

"Hardly."

"Ouch," said Al indignantly, rubbing his elbow, and trying to recover his dignity. "That bloody hurt."

"Serves you right."

Al shoved James's legs onto the floor and sat back down on the sofa next to him. "I take it that means that you are still quite keen on the big guy?"

"I still think he's the most amazing man in the world, pretty much," James said simply. He shrugged apologetically. "God, Al," he added, unable to help himself, "I couldn't live without him."

Al leaned in and kissed him. Apparently the shove was forgiven. "I know, Jamie." He was more serious now and gave a bit of a sigh. "If you want the truth, I'm not much better myself. Desperate for you, desperate for him. Like a lovesick puppy, for god's sake. Fucking pathetic for someone who never wanted a relationship, really, isn't it?"

"Oh, shut up," James said, lovingly.

"I just wish..." Al broke off.

"Let me guess. You're feeling in need of Laurie in a way that I just can't do for you, yeah?"

James had seen the growing desire and want in Al's face as he watched Laurie sometimes. The expression that told how much Al wanted to submit to Laurie, to do anything and everything Laurie asked of him. James couldn't entirely blame him; Laurie was bloody hot like that, and though James himself had no submissive side in the same way, he could certainly appreciate Al's wistfulness. Of course, Al could probably find a dozen men—or indeed women—willing to dominate him if he asked them; but James knew that even though Al enjoyed sex with all sorts of people, it would not be the same. What Al had just said about love was key. Laurie could give him something no one else could, precisely because of the way Al felt about him. He loved James, too; but though he was no submissive, James was also pretty sure he couldn't dominate his way out of a paper bag. Whereas Laurie...

"Jamie, you can take me any time, as you bloody well know. I think I was just showing that fairly loud and clear. But," admitted Al ruefully, "I am fucking desperate for Laurie to dominate me a bit. A bit? Hell, a lot."

"Then," said a new voice, "you had better get naked and on your knees in the next thirty seconds."

Both James and Al looked around guiltily. How they had not been aware of Laurie coming in, James couldn't say. And Laurie had managed the sort of unfortunate timing which was a real talent, waiting until he was being spoken about in explicit detail. Nonetheless, Al, after that one brief glance, was already stripping, his breathing quickening a bit as he pulled his T-shirt over messed hair and shoved his jeans and pants down and off his legs with his socks before sliding onto his knees. He clasped his hands firmly together at the small of his back, and bowed his head in front of Laurie, who strolled further into the room and kissed James hard and passionately. James felt his own heart beat a little faster. This was a version of Laurie which had been in very short supply since Brooke

Lingarten's newspaper article first broke; and James realised he had missed it almost as much as Al had. He wondered how long Laurie had been standing there; whether he had heard James's and Al's declarations of love for him. But Laurie couldn't have been in any doubt about that. It was hardly a secret, after all.

"So, Jamie," Laurie said, having kissed him with a thoroughness which left James's mouth tingling and his breath catching in his chest, "good day?"

"Not bad. Improving by the minute," James said truthfully.

Laurie gave him a little smile at this before turning his attention to Al. "As to you, little slut," he murmured, standing over the kneeling young man and putting one finger under his chin to raise his head so that they were looking at each other. "If you have something you want, you get on your knees and you come and ask me for it nicely. You don't go complaining to James. Do I make myself clear?"

The change in Al was fascinating. Gone was the usual version of James's friend and love already. It usually took him a little while to fall into subspace, but on this occasion he was clearly already there. His whole expression had changed to one of submission, but at the same time, James could see that Al's cock was beginning to harden once more. James couldn't entirely blame him; Laurie was hot when he was radiating this sort of dominating confidence.

"Yes, Sir."

Laurie made him keep his gaze for a long few seconds. "Good," he said at last. "Of course, I think you have some making up to do for talking about me behind my back—or trying to," he added with a quirk of the lips. He removed his finger from Al's face, and Al's head dropped immediately.

"Yes, Sir," he said again.

"Hmm." There was a thoughtful note in Laurie's voice as he considered his options. Then, clearly something came to him. He nodded. "Right. Into the bedroom with you. You can stand up, but you'll keep your hands behind your back and your eyes on the floor." Al obediently got to his feet. Laurie glanced over at James. "Coming, Jamie?" he asked, in a very different tone of voice to the forceful one he'd used with Al. Sensual, sexy. Equally promising, in its own way.

James found his mouth curling into a smile. "Oh yeah. Wouldn't miss it for the world."

The three of them moved into the bedroom. When they were there, Al went to get back on his knees, but Laurie stopped him with a hand to his arm.

"No. Stand there," he ordered.

Opening the wardrobe, he pulled out the belt of his dressing gown; then, with brisk efficiency, he used it to tie Al's hands together behind his back, curling it round his wrists several times before fastening it in a tight knot which would only get tighter if Al struggled. The belt was made of a soft material: it would not hurt, but it effectively bound Al's hands in place. James looked on with interest. This was something new. When Laurie had finished, he pushed Al towards the wall, until his back was against it. Then, deliberately, Laurie stepped very, very close to his lover, crowding his space, making clear the height and weight difference between them.

"We both know," Laurie said softly, "that I'm considerably stronger than you in the first place, brat. Now, with your hands tied like this, you're completely in my power. I could do anything I wanted with you, and you wouldn't be able to stop me, would you?"

"No, Sir." Al's voice was very quiet.

"I could push you face-first onto the bed and bugger you senseless and there would be nothing you could do but take it," Laurie murmured, remorselessly. "I could finger you, rubbing the tips of my fingers across your prostate over and over until you begged me to touch your cock and then ignore your pleading and do it some more, until you were barely able to speak with need." He moved closer still, so that their bodies were pressing up together. "Anything I wanted, Al. Does that turn you on?"

Al's head was back against the wall, and he was taking panting breaths, his eyes flickering shut.

"Oh god. Yes, Sir."

James felt the same way. He stroked his own burgeoning erection, sitting on the bed and watching Laurie give Al precisely what Al had admitted he'd been dying for. James grinned. Laurie himself didn't seem to be too averse to what he was doing, either.

"You might want to take those trousers off, James," Laurie added, without turning round. "Much more comfortable if you want to touch yourself." Damn it, how the hell did he know what James was doing when he wasn't looking? "Anyway," James's boyfriend continued, "Al might not be able to use his hands, but he has a very serviceable mouth still available. He seems to have been flapping it to you rather too much today already, so perhaps he can find a better use for it." He moved a step back from Al and pushed him towards the bed. "Go and suck James's cock for him, hmm? Put your mouth to a good purpose."

Al clambered onto the bed as James shrugged off his trousers and pants. Laurie removed his own underwear and trousers (and James could see from the erect state of Laurie's cock that all three of them were *definitely* getting off on this) and got onto the bed next to James, pulling James's top off and then wrapping an arm around him to kiss him some more. Al was clumsier than usual without the use of his hands, kneeling and then sliding his head into James's lap and beginning to lick and mouth his way over James's erection. Still, James, with Laurie snogging him and Al blowing him, couldn't help feeling that today was going in an extremely satisfactory direction. Laurie's kisses were always amazing; and Al was not only very accomplished with his mouth, but took such genuine pleasure in sucking someone off that it increased the enjoyment level proportionately. To see Al with his mouth around James's cock, you'd think that James was bestowing the favour, not receiving it.

As if to prove James's point, Al mumbled, "Love your cock, Jamie," around the area of James's groin, before he set more thoroughly to his task, taking the head and part of the shaft into his mouth.

James found his eyes drawn to the small of Al's back, where his hands were bound together; there was something inappropriately erotic about being serviced by someone in such a subservient state. James had a feeling he shouldn't enjoy it quite as much as he did...until he looked down and remembered how much Al himself was clearly enjoying himself.

"Yes," said Laurie, his eyes on Al also, "you love that. Don't you, you little slut?"

Al made a muted noise of agreement around James's erection, which shot sparks of sensation through James's body, making him groan in turn. Laurie began to run his fingers in little circles on Al's back, a gesture which made Al hum appreciatively, arching his back a little, as a cat might do. James wondered whether Al knew how those sounds went straight through him; suspected he did. But Al could not have been silent unless directly ordered to, James knew. It just wasn't in him. And James certainly wasn't complaining—the thrumming sensation of Al's noises was anything but unpleasant. With a final kiss for James, Laurie inched further down the bed, tracing the same light circles on Al, but on his arse, instead. Al was rocking back and forth now, his thighs pressed tightly together; James knew that if he could see Al's cock, it would be rock-hard.

"I think he likes that," he said to Laurie, casually, resisting with difficulty the temptation to thrust his own hips a little, pushing his cock further into Al's mouth.

"Oh, you think?" Laurie's voice was full of laughter.

James knew that the tips of Laurie's fingers would be barely touching Al's skin. So gentle as to be almost imperceptible. So gentle as to be almost unbearable. As if reacting to their conversation, Al began to suck harder, moving deeper down James's cock and drawing a sudden gasping breath from James. Apparently his lover had some tricks of his own to play.

"Shall I fuck him, Jamie?" Laurie asked. "Whilst he has his mouth round you?"

James shook his head. "Fuck him *onto* me," he said. "I'll lie underneath him, and he'll rut up against me as you take him." It would mirror what he and Al had been doing earlier, when they'd both been so close. But better. Naked. Al being buggered by Laurie. James with the weight of both of his lovers on top of him, and the feeling that they were both doing him. Al had made a little whining noise at James's words, and James and Laurie met each other's eyes and smiled. "He won't have any control," James went on. "Not with his hands tied. He'll be reliant on me to hold him against me, on you to rock him into me."

"Fuck," said Laurie quietly, betrayed into an unusual loss of control. "Jamie, you're—" He broke off, and leaned over to find the lube.

"After you with that," James said, as Laurie squeezed the lubricant onto his fingers. "I'm going to do Al and me, so we'll be all wet, sliding up against each other as you fuck him."

Al was still sucking on James, but he was moaning almost constantly now, little pleading noises. James watched Laurie slick his own cock and put slippery fingers to Al's hole. James himself had liberally doused one of his hands with lube, and he carefully pushed Al up from his cock with the other, balancing him. Al's eyes met his, pupils wide with lust.

"James, please," he whispered.

"Please what?"

"Do...oh god, do what you said. *Please.*"

Al was so beautiful like this, all needy and begging. James slid down underneath Al, reaching his sticky hand to Al's cock and drawing another groan out of his boyfriend. He stroked him until he was impossibly wet, then used the last of the lube on his own erection. Then he was lying underneath Al, and Laurie was above them, sliding an arm around Al's waist and pulling him back with a firm but careful motion onto his cock.

"Oh god, oh god, that feels so good. Laurie, Sir, James, please."

Al was already beginning to babble, as he always did. His body was warm against James's; his cock felt almost too good against James's own. James leaned up and kissed the words from Al's lips, and Al sighed with pleasure and kissed back. His eyes widened as he realised that he couldn't put his arms around James as he would usually do; he had clearly instinctively gone to move them and discovered that he could do no such thing. James put his hands on Al's hips, his arms alongside him, keeping him safely on top of him. It must feel strange to have no control over where your own body might go. And then Laurie thrust into Al, pushing him up against James, and James stopped caring about any of that. All that mattered was the feeling, and the knowledge that his two lovers were on top of him, fucking, and it felt so bloody good.

"You two are so fucking sexy underneath me," Laurie murmured, his thrusts slow and deliberate. He had his arms down by the side of their torsos; James turned one of his hands to run it up Laurie's muscular arm.

"And you're a bloody tease," James retorted, driven mad by Laurie's frustratingly leisurely pace combined with the heated words he was speaking. Al was rubbing against James, and James wanted more friction, damn it; faster, harder, more. Patience wasn't exactly his watchword, though years with Laurie had taught James more than he'd ever thought to know about it.

"You love it." Laurie's deep voice was so damn sensual. Sometimes James felt like he'd agree with anything Laurie said if he said it like that.

"Oh, but poor Al," James said, breathlessly, his lips quirking in amusement.

"'Poor Al' needs to learn not to talk about me behind my back," Laurie said, continuing his casual speed. "And you need to learn not to encourage him. Are you learning your lesson, James?"

James thought he was learning one lesson. He wasn't sure it was precisely the one that Laurie meant...but then again, perhaps it was. Laurie must have known when he chose to punish Al like this that it was hardly the cruellest thing he could do to him. Al had his head buried in James's neck and was licking and sucking at it and moaning into it almost at the same time, as if he couldn't stop himself from doing any of those things.

"Learning something," James said, bucking up under Al and making his lover moan that bit louder.

"Al, are you learning your lesson?" Laurie demanded. Al kept his head where it was and didn't answer. Laurie shifted his weight onto one arm and grabbed Al's hair, pulling him back up. "I said, little slut, are you learning your lesson?" he growled. "Or are you going to need to be punished more often?"

James looked at the glazed expression on Al's face, so full of desire. His boyfriend clearly wanted to beg to be punished more, but at the same time the submissive side of him called him to swear obedience; to tell Laurie he'd do whatever he asked whenever he asked it, to promise he'd behave.

"Please, Laurie. Please, Sir," Al managed, falling over the words. "Oh god, please."

Laurie laughed, and kissed his neck. "A slut, but our slut," he said. "So let's remind you of your place."

He let go of Al and began to fuck in more earnest, and it was James's turn to groan in relief. Al did too, so the noise come out almost in stereo. God, but Laurie was so hot, all dominant and demanding. He was gorgeous and sexy when he was being sensual and sweet, but Al did have a point: Laurie was definitely something incredible when he was like this.

"So hot, fuck," James said, beginning to pant as his cock got the precious friction against Al's.

Al was pleading and begging and pleading some more, and Laurie had this look of utter intensity on his face, as if nothing mattered but what he was doing to and with his lovers. Al came first, crying out, his head thrown back, and the sensation of his warm come against James's cock was enough to send James spiralling after him. Laurie's motions slowed now that his lovers had come, as if the speed had just been to get them off, and for himself he wanted something deeper and longer. He thrust hard and deep but not so fast, and James was beginning to come down from his orgasm by the time Laurie gave one quiet groan and started coming. Al, always slower to recover himself, was now panting against James's chest, still making little noises of pleasure, and James put one arm around Al, and reached the other up to hold Laurie's hip. Laurie looked at him, an expression of such naked adoration on his face that even James could not doubt it. Al had always insisted that Laurie worshipped James, but up until now, the last lingering memories of Laurie walking out had still haunted James.

"I love you," James tried to say, but his voice was cracked, and the words didn't form properly. He hoped that Laurie understood, nonetheless.

Then Laurie was sliding off and out of Al, down on one side of James, where he turned to kiss him. Al flopped clumsily to the other side, his head still tucked firmly into James's shoulder as if he could not bear to break the connection. His hands were still tied, but he made no complaint. As soon as he'd recovered himself a little, however, Laurie leaned over and painstakingly undid the knots he'd tied earlier. As the belt slipped off, the marks around Al's wrists were red and obvious, and James saw a slightly anxious look on Laurie's face as he looked at them. Al, however, merely gave them a little rub and then reached one hand out to Laurie's face, touching it gently.

"Thank you," he whispered, his expression open and trusting.

"You okay?" Laurie asked, his eyes on the marks.

Al smiled. "Am now," he said, sounding a strange combination of vulnerable and smugly satisfied. "Much, much better. Jamie?"

"Yeah, funny that," James acknowledged. "I could say the same."

Laurie's face twitched into a smile. "I'll admit that I've felt worse," he said. "You two are bloody gorgeous, by the way."

"Have I ever mentioned how sexy you are when you're all dominant?" James asked Laurie, suddenly realising that he might not have done. Being dominated was Al's thing, after all; the fact that it turned James on massively to watch the two of them at it was perhaps not so obvious.

"Mmm," agreed Al, nuzzling back into James's shoulder and kissing it with an open mouth.

James looked down at him and smiled. Al was always so tactile. Even after sex, he couldn't keep his mouth to himself—kissing, licking, and making small noises of contentment deep in his throat.

"And you, when you're not," he added to his other lover.

Al took advantage of having control back over his hands to run them all over James. James wasn't complaining, even when one of Al's hands moved further still, to stroke Laurie's chest.

"Feel so good," Al mumbled, wriggling up close against James's side.

"I just... I felt like such a pervert after what was written in the paper," Laurie confessed, leaning his forehead against James's and fuzzing Al's messy, sweaty hair with one of his hands.

Al chuckled, running his own hand further down Laurie's body and placing it gently over Laurie's spent cock. "Well, I hope you are," he said shamelessly.

James gave a snort of laughter at this, and even Laurie laughed.

"You know what I mean, though," he said. "The whole 'fetish for young men' thing."

"Yeah, and I prey on women, or something," Al pointed out.

"Thing is—I don't have a fetish for young men."

"No? Damn," Al teased.

And it was good to hear Al able to joke about it. So good.

Laurie leaned further over and kissed the side of Al's head. "No, I have a fetish for you two, specifically and solely. And yes, sometimes I have a fetish for making Al behave himself for one of the few times in his life."

"Someone's got to do it," James said immediately, unable to resist. Al bit into his neck in retaliation, and James poked him. "Oi, that hurt! Stop that!"

Laurie gave Al's arse a quick smack. "Behave, you."

"Sorry, James," Al said obediently, kissing the place he'd just sunk his teeth into.

"Point made, I think," James commented, tucking his arm around Al and giving him a squeeze.

"I'm not going to feel bad about it," Laurie said, quietly. "It doesn't look like I'm doing either of you any irreparable harm—"

"Hardly!" interjected Al.

"And so, as James said so pertinently the other week, our fucking business is no one else's fucking business," Laurie finished.

Al made a noise of sheer contentment, lifting his head and looking at Laurie. There was a soft expression on his face, similar to the one he wore when he was deep in subspace and yet not quite the same. This was not submissiveness. It was pure love. Nonetheless, when he spoke, it was typical Al.

"Well, Jamie," he said, "it takes him a while, but he gets there in the end, our bloke." Still, he kissed Laurie with a tenderness which belied the tenor of his words, and James knew from the way that Laurie responded that his boyfriends understood each other well enough.

"Though tell me if you want me to stop calling you a slut, Al," Laurie added, his hand on Al's face for a few seconds.

Al gave a mischievous grin. "But I am a slut," he said cheerfully. He stroked the hand on Laurie's cock back and forth a few times and rubbed himself up against the side of James's body in a meaningful fashion. "And when it comes to you and James," he murmured, "I am a total and utter cockslut. Want me to prove it?" Al's ability to be ready for sex even so soon after having it was really rather impressive. "Plus," Al added, effectively distracting him from that train of thought, "the filthy things you say turn Jamie on something pretty amazing, and I love watching him come apart listening to you."

James, who had not been expecting this, blushed. It was true, he acknowledged to himself, that Laurie talking dirty in that deep, sensual voice of his got him horny very, very quickly. However, Al was not supposed to have noticed—and certainly not supposed to have commented on it.

"Shut up," he said quickly, giving his boyfriend a shove.

Al's look at him was wicked. "Call me a liar," he challenged.

James grinned. "I've been calling you a liar regularly for the last sixteen years," he retorted. "But you might have a point on this occasion."

"Um," added Al, a little more seriously, "but if you could avoid ever using the word 'whore' I'd be grateful." James and Laurie both looked at him, and he looked away. "Just...when I was attacked..." he mumbled— and said no more.

James bit his lip. Al had been beaten and orally raped by a group of men who called him a whore over and over as they did so. It was hardly surprising that he felt so strongly about it. The three of them mentioned it rarely, but there was always a certain awareness of it between them. Earlier that evening, Laurie had, James noticed, avoided mentioning the possibility that he might force Al to suck him off when he had suggested things which he might do to a bound and powerless Al. Al had coped amazingly after the experience, but there was no need to remind him unnecessarily of one of the worst moments of his life.

"Yes," said Laurie, the same understanding and sympathy showing in his voice, "I can do that." His tone changed. "Anything for you, brat," he said.

"Of course, call me *that* and I'll feel the need to live up to it," Al said slyly, glancing sideways at him.

Laurie laughed. "Trust me. You already do."

James jerked up, something suddenly stirring in his mind. He didn't know what had reminded him, but somehow listening to Laurie call Al a brat, it had all come back. Hel's article. Laurie hadn't been told about that yet.

"Fuck, Laurie doesn't know!" he exclaimed.

They'd been so...distracted, as it were...that it hadn't occurred to either Al or James to mention the article. Which said a lot, James reflected, about how much they'd needed to see the old Laurie back again. Now it had occurred to him, however, he couldn't believe that he—and especially that Al—hadn't thought to mention it earlier. Both the others looked at him in surprise, clearly not following his drift.

"Last time someone said that, it was a pretty awful experience," Laurie commented wryly. "Talk about ways to break the moment."

"What're you talking ab—oh," Al said, having a light-bulb moment.

James grinned. "Another article," he told Laurie. "This one, though, might be a little bit better. She sent him a preview."

Laurie sat up, looking interested. "Hel Gerrard come through for you?" he asked Al.

James snorted. "She pretty much had sex with him on the page," he said. "Hang on." He swung his legs out of bed. "I'll go and get it for you."

Laurie read his way through the article in silence, looking up at Al occasionally with a little smile. James, watching him, could make an educated guess as to whereabouts Laurie had reached by the expressions on his face. Early on, there was a nod of appreciation as to Hel's description of the films. A smile, which James suspected related to the comment about himself and Laurie. A shake of the head—that would be about the comment Al had made to Brooke. Later, a moment of tenderness which James was pretty sure mirrored his own, reading about the dates Al had left behind. Finally, Laurie spoke.

"It seems you made an impression, then," he commented.

James could see that Al's eyes were anxious, even now, as they looked at Laurie. He knew that his boyfriend still felt bad that he had been the unintentional cause of Laurie's distress. And there was another level to his anxiety, too. Al knew that Laurie knew of Hel Gerrard as a critic. He would be able to judge more accurately the importance of this article, especially given the strength of its backing.

"What do you think?"

"This is a preview copy, you said? It comes out tomorrow?" Laurie took a few seconds to consider. "I'd give it two days."

"Two days for what?" Al asked.

"Before the production company are on the phone, begging for your new film," Laurie said, smiling at him.

James raised his eyebrows. "She's that important?"

"To a production company the size of Al's? Yes," Laurie said definitively. "Bigger British companies would take some notice of her, given her reputation and the magazine this is going out in. Al's will be falling over itself." He glanced sideways at Al. "So might others, you know."

"I doubt it." Al didn't look bothered by his doubts, though. "Anyway, this lot have done all right for me. Can't really blame them for their reaction, in the circumstances. I just hope you're right about their next response."

"I am." Laurie pulled a face. "Won't get rid of all the Internet crap, of course. That's much more interesting than the truth."

"To be honest," James said, "there's quite a lot of back and forth going on out there as it is, even before this. It isn't all that one-sided. What?" he demanded, as the others stared accusingly at him. "It's not like neither of you have been looking, is it? There's a strong pro-Al group out there, though I swear to god even you can't have had sex with quite so many people as seem to be saying you have."

"You'd be surprised." Al grinned. "No, seriously, I've really never been quite as prolific as even you seem to 've thought. And the last year has been woeful, frankly, in terms of numbers." His smile turned smug. "In terms of quality, best yet, mind you," he admitted.

"Surprising thing is there's pretty much nobody claiming you've assaulted them personally, though," James added.

Al grimaced at this. "Like Hel Gerrard said, mostly when people say it, it's because it's true. Fuck it, even Brooke didn't actually claim I did anything to her. She just managed to imply it without a single word I could do her for."

"But at least if public record is disputing the original claims, that should be a good thing," James said, looking at Laurie.

"Oh, definitely," Laurie agreed. He looked through the article again and then at Al. "Al, love, I'm so glad. You deserve this."

Al always claimed to love praise, but it wasn't true. Genuine praise of this nature embarrassed him immensely. His usual, apparently arrogant, responses tended to be to cover up his discomposure.

"No," he said quietly. "But I'll take it. With any luck it'll take the pressure off you two, as well."

James shrugged. "I didn't have much. Worse in Year Thirteen."

"And I'm seeing mine through. I might always," Laurie said, not quite able to keep the note of regret entirely out of his voice, "be seen as the lecturer who molests his male students, but if that's what I have to put up with to keep you two, it's worth it."

"You won't be," Al said quickly; then, more slowly, he added, "but that's...maybe one of the nicest things you've ever said."

"Yes," James agreed.

Laurie swallowed hard and reached one hand out to each of them. "I suddenly woke up," he said quietly, "and realised that you are the most important things in my life. Much more than my job, my reputation. If I'd kept those, and lost you two—even one of you, Al—it wouldn't have been worth the exchange."

"Oh."

Al was looking away, and James knew there were tears in his eyes. His sappy best friend had never been great at hiding his emotions. Al had known it, too—it was partly why he'd always been open about who he was, knowing that he wouldn't have been able to disguise it very brilliantly even if he'd tried. The other part had been sheer bloody mindedness: Al's parents had always told him he wasn't good enough, and where in another child that might have brought out an apologetic tendency to be ashamed and hide who they were, Al had been the more determined to be precisely the person he chose to be, without fear or favour. James kicked him, long-time boyish friendship overcoming the lover in him, and Al blinked back the tears and pulled a face at James.

"Yeah," said James bracingly, "don't make that face at me, Allie. I feel exactly the same way, even if I can't make nice speeches like Laurie."

"Will you two ever grow up?" Laurie demanded.

"Probably not." Al wiped his eyes with his hand and smiled at Laurie. "Anyway, you've just pretty much said you love us anyway, so you've not exactly given us masses of incentive."

Laurie raised his hands. "I can't stand you! I hate the pair of you! I want you out of my sight! Why do I get the feeling that neither of you are convinced?"

James leaned into his big boyfriend, kissing the side of his face to prevent either of the others seeing that his own eyes weren't entirely dry. Al, earlier—*desperate for you, desperate for him*—now Laurie—*you are the most important things in my life.* Then there was the article—Hel Gerrard, a journalist who probably wouldn't have looked at Al's work had it not been for the scandal and Gemma, but who was now praising James's boyfriend to the skies. Laurie hadn't even known about that, yet he'd come home tonight his old self. And James? James was surrounded by the men he loved, the men he now knew beyond doubt loved him.

"Maybe because you weren't really trying to convince us?" Al suggested, rolling onto James in order to get closer to Laurie.

"Maybe so," Laurie admitted. His arms went around the two younger men, and he held them tightly. "That might just be so."

About the Author

P.A. Friday fails dismally to write one sort of thing and, when not writing erotica and erotic romance of all sexualities, may be found writing articles on the Regency period, pagan poetry, or science fiction. She loves wine and red peppers, and loathes coffee and mushrooms.

Email: penfriday@gmail.com

Website: www.penelopefriday.com

Twitter: @penelopefriday

Facebook: www.facebook.com/penelopefriday

Other books by this author

All About the Boy

Math Series

Love Plus One

One Plus One

Also Available from NineStar Press

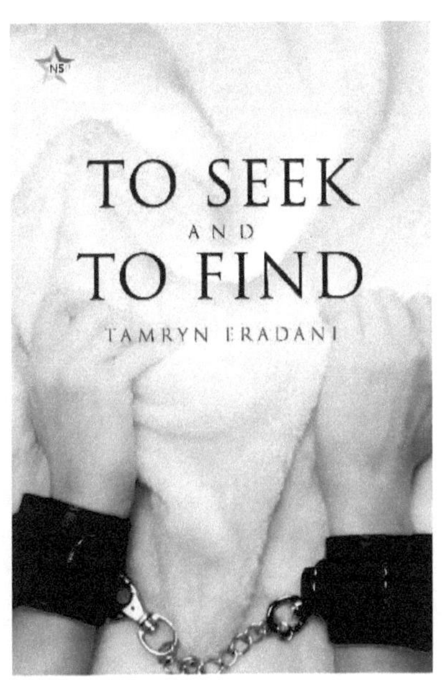

Connect with NineStar Press

www.ninestarpress.com

www.facebook.com/ninestarpress

www.facebook.com/groups/NineStarNiche

www.twitter.com/ninestarpress

www.tumblr.com/blog/ninestarpress